DREW

JASPER SPRINGS

BOOK THREE

BY EVIE RILEY

Drew

An MM Bad Boy Rockstar Romance

Jasper Springs

Book Three

Copyright © 2024

Evie Riley

Second Edition

ISBN: 978-1-77357-686-2

Published by Naughty Nights Press LLC

Cover Art By Willsin Rowe

DREW

A wounded heart.

A shared love of music.

A whirlwind romance with the power to heal.

Drew Axel is ready for a change after his famously public split from famed actor, Rozen Lane. When he stops to perform in his childhood town, getting back to his roots, the last thing Drew expects to find is love. Especially with a fellow Swiftie.

Taylor Meade has two loves in his life: His floral shop and his favorite female singer. Despite being in the business of weddings, Taylor has given up on finding the perfect man to fit into his Swift-inspired dreams. That is, until he wakes up hungover in rockstar Drew Axel's tour bus.

As fate draws Drew and Taylor closer, they both soon discover music isn't the only thing they have in common. Will Drew give up a life of glitz and glamor for his wildest dreams? Or will Taylor find himself fighting more than just Drew's bad boy reputation?

Readers seeking a bad boy rockstar romance with forced proximity set in a cozy little town may find this story ticks those boxes. While Drew and Taylor may have cameos in future stories, each book in this series can be read as a standalone.

CHAPTER ONE

Drew

IT'S GOOD TO be home.

I sighed as I parked my bus at the edge of the parking lot of *M's Place,* a tiny little hole-in the wall bar in the small town of Jasper Springs.

It'd been nearly twenty years since I left the quaint place, after scoring my first big time record deal. Though it was home, it didn't feel like home anymore, not without my parents who no longer lived here, or with the new buildings and shops that replaced the old ones I once remembered.

I sat for a moment and appreciated the view of the sunset behind the trees, the way the light kissed the pavement, glinting off the metal of my *Axe 2 Grind* lanyard hanging in the window.

While my bandmates and I were on hiatus so we could focus on our solo projects, I was excited at the idea of traveling to more local spots to perform instead of the bigger venues the band normally played at. Which meant I'd be taking the bus across the country to hit all the little dives, diners, and practically dungeons in my path from LA to Pittsburgh.

The fresh air and change of scenery would be good for me, or so I told myself.

Though perhaps it wasn't just a need for a change of scenery that had me chomping at the bit, ready to jump on a bus by myself and head for the hills. If I was being honest, it might have had something to do with *America's Sexiest Man Alive,* Rozen Lane. My cheating bastard of an ex-boyfriend.

"You gonna just sit there like a fucking lump, Axel, or are you gonna get yourself checked in?" The grumble of my long-time friend and manager, Helena "Howler" Dryfuss bit as she stopped just behind the driver seat.

I sighed, flipping the key to turn the engine off, then turning in my chair to look at her. Okay, maybe I wasn't taking this trip just by myself. Howler would be with me no matter where I went, like a bad case of poison ivy.

"Can I just have a minute, Howler? Christ, I haven't been home in like, a lifetime. Maybe I just want to, you know, process shit?" I growled.

Helena shot me a scathing look, her bright blue eyes full of disdain and annoyance.

"You had sixteen hours to process, baby. Therapy time is over. Now get your ass in gear, and let's get set up. The show must go on."

I dropped my hand from the steering wheel, letting out a sigh as the door opened, deciding perhaps Helena was right.

Sitting in my bus moping was not doing me any favors at the moment, and if there was one thing that I was capable of doing that would take my mind off Rozen, it was performing. So, I grabbed my white electric guitar from the couch in front of the door, flashing Helena a bright, white-toothed smile as I cocked my head, shedding my inner homeboy and channeling the man people paid to see. The man I'd been for the last twenty years.

"Right, of course."

CHAPTER TWO

Drew

M'S PLACE WAS fairly packed for a Tuesday night, but then again, it wasn't like most of the inhabitants in this town had a lot of options for nightlife. Not unless they got in their cars and took off for the city, of course.

While I'd been used to crowds pretty much everywhere I went, being the frontman of my band and boy toy to *America's Sexiest Man Alive*, I had to admit the atmosphere of M's Place was a breath of fresh air. No one bum-rushed me at the door for an autograph, or tried to break into my bus. It was almost as if they didn't know who I was, or if they did, they just didn't give a shit, and a part of me was engaged by that. It reminded me of those first years I'd been on the road with my boys, trying to get my name out there. Trying to get people to notice me, to pay attention to a skinny-jeans clad skeleton with a mop of hair who looked like the boy next door instead of a fucking rock star.

At least until I'd started to invest in my ink.

Now, I'm a hell of a lot bigger, thanks to a steady diet of protein shakes and grass Rozen had me on for the last year and all the workouts in between. I wasn't exactly small potatoes before I met the man, but I bet I couldn't even get my leg in the top of my old skinny-jeans now.

DREW

I tuned up my guitar for my first song, watching the crowd who barely seemed to notice me standing there on stage.

I sucked in a deep breath and grabbed the mic, introduced myself as Drew Axel from Axe 2 Grind, and thanked them for letting me perform for them, something I used to do a hell of a lot more in the beginning when I used to play places like this. Nowadays, Axe 2 Grind was on a tight schedule. I barely got to do meet and greets anymore, something else I appreciated having the ability to do on this tour.

While a good bit of people turned to face me, intrigued enough likely by the name, I could see I hadn't captured *everyone*'s attention.

I will soon enough.

I caught Howler's gaze from the other side of the room, giving me the thumbs up to start my set. I strummed my guitar, the vibration in my fingers a welcome sensation as I struck the chords. The opening riff of Taylor Swift's *Blank Space* echoed in the air as the music from sound check accompanied me. It still felt weird to perform with my guitar without my bandmates, but there was a sort of rush to it too. It was just me.

And while that would have been scary in any other situation, on stage... that's where I was at my best. That's where I came *alive*.

Helena had tried to get me to stick to the formula and perform mostly *Axe 2 Grind* hits, but quite honestly, I was tired of performing the same old songs day in and day out.

I wanted something different, something new.

Covering Taylor Swift's pop songs was definitely not what A2G fans will expect.

I scanned the crowd, looking for one person in the crowd who I could pick out to perform to.

DREW

Most people didn't know that was my trick. The magazines always talked about how good I was live. When I was just starting out, I made it a point to find one person in every crowd, and I played for *them.* Usually, it was cocky assholes who thought they were too good to be there, dragged by friends or partners against their will to put up with my "noise."

If I could sway them, if I could pull them in, then I did my job.

And it seemed to work for the last twenty years.

My gaze settled on a man off to the left who was about two rows away. He looked visibly uncomfortable, which was perfect for me. If I could get this guy up and dancing, or at least nodding to my music, then I did my job.

It also didn't hurt that he was pretty attractive, despite his deer in the headlights look.

Actually, if I'm being honest, it only

adds to his appeal. I'll give that man something to look wide-eyed about, that's for sure.

"Nice to meet you, where you been?" I drawled as I made eye contact. He looked back and forth, as if I could be singing to someone else, so I zeroed in my gaze as I straightened my back, squaring my shoulders as I continued to sing. "I could show you incredible things," I sang, channeling the persona I usually took on stage.

Bold, confident, sexy, and maybe a little reckless. That's who Drew Axel was to the masses.

I crooned through the lyrics as I let my fingers slide over the frets, closing my eyes as the rhythm took me. My mind wandered as the words poured out of me of their own volition and I sang on about forever and going down in flames.

Like always, there was a hurricane of emotion swirling in my stomach as I felt the depth of the lyrics I covered.

My own songs didn't turn on the faucet anymore, they'd become less about me and more about what sells. I can't remember the last time I wrote a banger that really accessed your fucking feels.

But Taylor Swift did a really good job of that. Accessing my feels, I mean.

Plus her love life is about as sordid as mine, so if the shoe fits...

As I opened my eyes, I saw my target staring back at me with a look that was some cross between awe and lust, and I know I have him.

I crooned on about the high being worth the pain as I stroked my chords, spinning around as the music fills me. My legs opened as I took my trademark cocky stance, my dark hair falling in my eyes as my whole body practically convulses as I covet the guitar in my hands.

"Got a long list of ex-lovers," I scream-sang as I met his gaze. My cock twitched behind my guitar, which only fed my drive.

I rocked my guitar as I spun around, the heat of the lights spreading like wildfire through me as I ripped out the bit about players and the game. When I was facing the crowd again, I saw Mr. I Don't Belong Here staring at me like I was the only man in the room.

I smirked as I continued to play my heart out, never breaking my gaze.

Because as far as I was concerned, I was only playing for him.

CHAPTER THREE

Taylor

THE LAST THING I wanted to do after a long week of back to back orders was go out for a drink. I knew most of the guys my age would be all about shirking their responsibilities and jumping at a chance to get their drink on, especially with someone like Giselle.

Whether she's taken or not...

But me, I wasn't most guys. I knew that sounded cliché, but it was true. I'd much rather curl up on my couch and watch cringey rom-coms or scroll through florist TikToks while I have a self-care night instead of going out. But Giselle, bless her heart, would not take no for an answer.

Especially because her favorite rockstar, Drew Axel, was performing tonight at the local dive bar everyone in Jasper Springs flocked to.

I didn't grow up in Jasper Springs like Giselle, though from the stories she'd told me, I am not sure I'd have wanted to. The town of Jasper Springs itself was pretty small. The high school was built up of Jasper Springs, Deer Park, and Paradise residents, but the graduating class was still barely two hundred people. I couldn't imagine being that close to my classmates.

When I was in a senior in high school—a whopping seven years ago—I was a loner. I had a few friends, but after my break-up with my ex, when I moved to Jasper Springs, I lost contact with them. Nothing like moving to prove who your real friends are.

But I was determined to do this adult dream thing on *my* terms—and a small town like Jasper Springs was perfect for my ultimate dream: to own a flower shop that would put the Hallmark movie flower shops to shame.

I was still a long way from my goal, but I was here. I was the proud owner of *Taylor Made Bouquets*. I was living my dream... sort of.

The wedding scene wasn't as lively as I'd hoped in a small town, but despite that, I still kept the shop open, even if most of my sales were for funeral arrangements or graduations.

When I moved to Jasper Springs, Giselle was one of the first people I met. Long, leggy, and tanned with her dark hair swept back into a ponytail that screamed "Hamptons Honey", she'd taken it upon herself to bring a literal plate of cookies to my doorstep. Which technically, was across the street at the time.

I won't lie, I was worried she'd take our polite interaction the wrong way. Most women mistake my politeness for interest. Giselle said it was due to my lack of assertiveness, and my shyness. People didn't just *assume* you were gay.

But it wasn't something I advertised either.

What was I supposed to do?

Wear a sign that says "This Machine Only Takes Dick"?

No, thank you.

Not to mention, it wasn't like I had a ton of experience with men. Probably not as much as I should have for a twenty-five year old gay man.

My list of ex-lovers was pretty slim. I'd dated a couple guys in high school, but clearly I'd put more into the relationship slash situationship than my partners, including my longest relationship, my ex Zack.

Who left me for bigger, better things.

Though it might also be because I wasn't *assertive* enough in making my interest and affection clear, according to Giselle, who next to my other friend, Julie—who I also met when I moved to Jasper Springs and hit it off with immediately—was probably one of the smartest individuals I knew. I'd never been able to talk about my love of cock with anyone until I met them. Both women just had this comforting air about them. It was easy to open up to people when you weren't worried you were going to be judged or left behind.

I'd been trying to work on the assertiveness thing. I'd listened to audiobooks. I'd meditated. I'd even done those stupid exercises in the mirror. And I thought I was shifting my mindset, that I could most certainly tell people *no,* or walk with faked confidence into a room, if only because I thought if I made that sort of change in my life, my business would prosper too.

Fake it till you make it, right?

But somehow I'd caved like a wilted sunflower when Giselle *begged* me to come with her to M's Place so she could see Drew Axel perform tonight.

I knew who *Axe 2 Grind* were, if only because it was Giselle's and Julie's favorite band. I preferred Taylor Swift, the most prolific artist of our fucking generation.

I bet Drew Axel doesn't write his own songs like Taylor does. Probably too busy partying on his big tour bus or making an ass of himself in the public eye.

Giselle curled close to me as I took a sip of my wine. I didn't expect top shelf vino at a place like M's Place, but I had to admit the rosé wasn't all that bad.

We'd managed to score a seat close to the stage, as Giselle insisted it was pivotal we arrived early because she thought the show would be sold out, and the place wasn't all that big to begin with.

I hated to admit she was right. The place was packed with the karaoke crowd prior, being as M's was well known for its karaoke and bar bingo crowd that met once a month, and naturally they'd booked Drew Axel's show immediately following their signature event. Many of the regulars stayed through the rockstar's set, mixed in with fans like Giselle, and I'm sure several other significant others and gay besties who were dragged against their will to this show.

But the moment those lights dimmed, and Drew strummed his guitar, something in the world shifted.

I recognized the riff, albeit it was faster, and darker sounding than I was used to, but when he opened his eyes, bright green framed by thick black eyeliner, and looked at me—no, *gazed* at me—like I was the only person in the room, my entire body heated like a flame.

Not to mention my overzealous cock decided that was a good time to remind me no one had looked at me like that ever, and he liked the attention as much as I did.

I shifted in my seat as Giselle removed her arm from my shoulders, standing instead and moving to the music. I was thankful for her move, if only because the last thing I wanted was for my friend to discover my surprise erection in public. We were close, but not that close. I nonchalantly adjusted myself, feigning the façade of comfortability as I shifted in my seat, crossing my legs, and squeezing tight to try and rein in my burgeoning hardness.

What the fuck is wrong with me?

DREW

In my peripheral vision, Giselle swayed, but I couldn't focus on her. I could only focus on the way Drew Axel held his guitar, on the way pink and blue lights drew highlights along the curve of his ass in his ripped jeans, on the way his hair fell in his eyes, and the way he kept fucking *staring* at me like he was undressing me with his damn eyes.

My cock twitched in my khakis, all too eager and excited.

The entire set was like that, from his opening cover of *Blank Space* to his ending cover of *Wonderwall.*

Finally relieved that the show was over, I stood up way too fast, suddenly dizzy, no doubt from all the blood rushing from my head to my... other head.

Fucking hell, why won't you just go down!

"Well, that was fun. I—"

"Sweet G, is that you?" A deep, smooth voice cut through my words, and suddenly there was a rush of people knocking into us.

"Only in the flesh," she chirped excitedly as I turned to see who she was talking to, my eyes widening as I realized it was the man himself.

Drew fucking Axel.

I did a double take, looking from one to the other. I knew she liked the guy, I mean *Axe 2 Grind* was her favorite band, but she'd never once said she *knew* the guy.

Just how did she know a rockstar?

Was my friend keeping groupie secrets?

Drew pulled Giselle into a hug as several other women tugged at the holes of his muscle shirt, clamoring for an autograph. When he pulled back, he grabbed their photos, signed them—and a couple stomachs too—and took his pictures.

Giselle didn't seem put off, but the

longer the guy stood there, the longer I stared, which wasn't helping my current situation. In fact, it only made me more focused on *leaving* this seventh circle of hell.

When the girls had scampered off, he turned his attention on Giselle again, who was now threading her arm through mine, squeezing me once again with excitement.

"It's been what, at least twenty years? You still look as gorgeous as the day I met you," he said, flashing her with a smile that was far too cheesy for my liking. A strange pang of jealousy ransacked me as my cock twitched, remembering how he'd looked at *me* like that.

But I knew it was all for show. Men like Drew Axel didn't like guys like me. We were just numbers and figures to them, and they'd sell whatever they needed to in order to get their hands in our wallets.

"Giselle, I think we should—"

"And you look ten times better," she

teased, and the man actually had the audacity to laugh like they truly were old chums.

"Let me buy you and your man a drink," Drew said, sliding his hand in his pockets.

"Oh, I'm not her man," I said reflexively. "I'm just the poor soul she held against his will to come here."

I watched as Drew's lips curled into a smirk, and my cock twitched.

I really need to get the hell out of here.

Giselle poked me in the ribs. "Oh, don't even start, Taylor. You know you loved it," she teased.

Drew cocked his head to the side, his gaze appraising me with interest.

"Taylor, huh? Not a fan?" he asked, clicking his tongue.

"Don't take it personally, *Drew*," I said, a strange sense of confidence rising up in me. "You're just, not my type," I said.

His green eyes sparkled in the light as

he chuckled darkly, and I realized all at once I hadn't said music.

"Of music, I mean," I clamored, trying to cover up the weird flirty-not flirty dig I'd just taken at a damn *celebrity*.

What the fuck is wrong with me tonight?

"Your words wound me so, *Taylor.*" The way he said my name, made my literal hairs stand on edge, goosebumps pricking my skin.

And then he turned from me, shunning me no doubt for my stupid comment, focusing his pearly white smile on Giselle.

"So how about that drink, G?" he said. "You and *Taylor* up for shooting the shit?"

And like the little minx she was, Giselle decided to really make my night a living hell, when she answered, "Taylor and I would love a drink, wouldn't we, Taylor?"

CHAPTER FOUR

Taylor

ONE DRINK FOR Giselle and Drew turned into three drinks, and I was not quite drunk enough to deal with either of them.

The two went on and on about their time in school together—apparently the rockstar was from the area—droning on about a catch up like a badly written episode of Reunion before it was canceled.

I'd debated leaving the two of them to stare into each other's eyes for the rest of the night, convinced neither would notice I was gone.

Which is why I'd taken it upon myself to get up and go to the bathroom, when really I just needed someone to commiserate with.

So I called Julie, naturally.

"Hey," I said when she answered.

"Hey," she said, clearly surprised by my late night call. "Are you okay?"

"Yeah, I'm fine. You'll never guess where I'm at," I said.

"The shop?" Julie teased.

"Nope, Giselle cornered me into going to this stupid concert tonight at M's Place," I said dejectedly.

"You mean Drew Axel's concert?" Julie's voice elevated, and I could hear the faint echo in the background from the depth of her excitement.

"Yeah, that concert. Apparently, they know each other, like went to school together. We're having drinks, and—"

"Shut up, Taylor! You are *not* having a drink right now with my teenage dream," she gushed, completely guffawing over what I'd just said.

What was everyone's deal?

Yeah the guy was hot, but what else did he have to offer?

Why was everyone so into this guy?

Maybe it's the tattoos.

Maybe it's the way he holds his guitar.

Or the way he looks at you when he sings.

I forced away the thoughts threatening to bring my cock back to life. I'd only just gotten myself to soften, no thanks to thoughts about the most mundane shit possible.

Thoughts of taxes and funeral arrangements will kill any erection.

"Not really. It's pretty much just the Giselle and Drew show right now. I doubt they even notice I've left to call you."

"You *have* to get me an autograph. I

will love you forever!" She squealed.

"I thought you already loved me!" I said, teasing her back. Though a part of me was incensed at her words.

"I do... I didn't mean... I just... I'm stuck here working overnight, and you're drinking with my idol, and I'm having major fear of missing out right now, Tay."

I rolled my eyes as I slowly sauntered away from the bathrooms, my gaze falling on Drew where he sat at the bar. The fans had mostly gone, and the bar itself looked to be clearing out, likely because it was nearly one in the morning, and last call would be soon.

I watched as Giselle smiled, and as Drew ran his tattooed fingers down her arm, smiling in return.

Something about the gesture felt intimate, sweet almost, and the way he looked at her like she was the brightest star in the room, stirred an ache in my own heart.

DREW

I wished someone would touch me and look at me like that. Like the way he'd looked at me when he sang *Blank Space*.

"I know, I'm sorry, it's just... I'm having an off day today. This isn't really my scene, you know?" I said as I turned around, leaning against the wall.

"Newsflash, you know you *are* allowed to have fun, right?" Julie said.

"I don't know if drinking and rock music are my idea of a good time," I admitted.

"Rather be one with your flowers and reruns of Gilmore Girls?" she teased.

"You know it," I said. My gaze flashed to the clock on the wall that read twelve forty-five, before settling on the door of the bathroom, and I figured now was as good a time as any to do my business and wrap up this night and collect my date. We'd definitely stayed long enough, and I needed to get home so I could get some sleep before work tomorrow.

"I've got to go, Jules, I think its time to pay the check and peace the fuck out," I said as I hung up, making my way into the bathroom.

Surprisingly, at that time of the night the bar was thinning out, and there wasn't anyone else in the space except me. So, I took my time. I'd just unzipped my pants when the door opened.

The sound of clamoring boots made my body tense.

But when I saw familiar ripped jeans and a handful of tattoos, my body relaxed.

"Apologies if I'm boring you to tears," Drew Axel drawled as he slowly unzipped his pants.

I gripped my cock a little tighter, shaking off the remains of my piss if only because I was far too tempted to focus on other things.

And I didn't want Drew to get the wrong idea.

Why do I care what he thinks of me?

I barely know the guy.

"You're not boring me," I said.

Drew smirked, his green gaze sparkling with mischief.

"This just... isn't my cup of tea, that's all," I said.

Drew scoffed, his gaze dipping to where I held myself, and I felt my cheeks redden. It certainly wasn't abnormal to check out the dick of the guy next to you, but what was abnormal was the way my cock instantly hardened under Drew's gaze.

I shifted my stance as I tucked my hardened cock back in my pants.

"It's not mine either, you know. It's just part of the job," Drew scoffed, his gaze traveling back up my body to my face once more.

A mixture of mortification and excitement coursed as I did exactly what I knew I shouldn't.

I looked down. So sue me.

I watched as Drew's hand stroked his shaft, slower than a man who'd just taken a piss probably should. I swallowed harshly, not because of feelings of inadequacy. There were plenty of assholes out there with bigger dicks than me, and that never really affected me in any negative ways.

But it wasn't Drew's size that had me spiraling.

It was the piercings.

He had a fucking Jacob's Ladder.

Why was that hot?

Why was I still looking like a fucking perv?

"Yeah, well, we all do what we have to do, right?" I said, probably a little too harshly as I zipped my pants and headed to the sink.

Drew grunted in response, before answering, "Right."

And with that, I was off to collect Giselle, and get the hell out of that place.

DREW

I needed my bed in the worst way.

"Hey, you ready?" I said as I reached the bar, my words forcing Giselle to look at me.

"Oh… but we just got started…" Giselle pouted.

"It's like, one in the morning, Giselle. You know we both have work, and a life to get back to," I said as I signaled for Miguel to bring the check.

"Yeah, I should call it a night too," Drew said, approaching us from behind. He leaned his hand against the bar as if to steady himself between Giselle and I, the motion knocking his legs right into mine, almost knocking me down in the process.

I grabbed the bar for steadiness myself, as I flashed a glare at him.

What the hell?

Miguel presented me the check, and I sighed, reaching in my pocket for my wallet if only to hurry this along. So, I was quite surprised when Drew literally plucked it right out of my hands—his fingertips brushing the back of my knuckles as he did so, which only relit the fire I'd felt earlier watching him. And moments ago during our weird tense moment.

His fingertips on my skin were surprisingly... soft, slightly cold from the fresh washing in the sink of the bathroom, smooth with the faint sheen of bar soap.

"Absolutely not, this one is on me," Drew said, flashing me with a smirk as he autographed the check.

"Thanks," Giselle said as she clutched my arm, her warmth radiating through me as my gaze caught Drew's.

"Don't worry about it. Knight in Shining Armor here can get it next time," he said with a wink as he pushed away from the bar.

Heat threatened to flush my cheeks

once more, so I turned away from the rockstar in question.

"Goodbye," I growled, much harsher than I'd meant to.

I sped out of M's Place toward my car, toting a clumsy Giselle like a child on a leash.

"Why do you have to be such a killjoy?" she pouted.

I opened the car door for her, helping her inside.

"I'm not a killjoy, I just... I'm trying to take care of you," I said. "Make sure no one takes advantage of you," I said.

Giselle laughed. "Drew was right, you are a knight in shining armor," she giggled.

"No, your knight in shining armor is Aaron, remember?" I said as I rounded the driver's side of the car.

Giselle sighed. "Aaron would understand catching up with an old friend," she said, as I started the car up.

"Mhmmm," I said as I looked in my review mirror.

"Besides, I'm not Drew's type. Not by a long shot." She laughed.

"He's a rockstar, I'm pretty sure everyone is his type," I chirped.

Giselle laughed again.

"You know he is into men, right?" She chuckled.

I nearly hit the brakes on the car.

I knew he'd been in the tabloids about a supposed break up with Rozen Lane, but I didn't believe most of the stories. In fact, most of the tabloids reported on him leaving clubs and houses of *women* of all professions, actresses, heiresses, models. One random rumor of being with the hottest man alive did not make the man gay.

Right?

I shoved down the part of me that wanted to believe a man like Drew actually preferred dick.

DREW

My luck is never that good.

"I think you are drunk and not thinking clearly," I said as I drove along the quiet drag toward our neighborhood.

"I think you're just afraid to admit you like him," she teased.

"His show wasn't bad, I'll give him that. But you can't *like* someone you just met. Life isn't a romance novel," I said as I pulled up to her driveway, behind Aaron's car.

I shifted the car into park, and she shot me a soft smile before reaching for her door.

"Thanks, Taylor. I'll text you in the morning," she said softly.

I waited until I'd watched her head into the house, until the door had closed behind her and the lights were turned on.

I sighed in the quiet of my car. I hadn't meant to sound so disillusioned, but it was the truth. No matter how badly I wanted to buy into the fantasy of a hot, sexy rockstar who would literally rock my world, I knew that life didn't work like that, and even if it did...

Even if it did, those sorts of stories were far and few between, and they never happened to a twenty-five year old gay florist with confidence issues living in Small Town USA.

I put my car in reverse, and I decided to put all thoughts of Drew Axel and tonight's events out of my mind.

CHAPTER FIVE

Taylor

MY ALARM WENT off like it always did, at six fifteen in the morning, blaring like a siren. Most of the time, I was in bed by ten, and thoroughly rested, and I'd rise, stretch and be about my normal routine. But after getting less than a good six hours of sleep, I was not in the mood for my alarm and it's havoc this morning.

I reached for the phone, fumbling to grasp it and shut off the maddening sound. Just as I managed to do so, the phone vibrated in my hand, pinging with a sound I knew too well.

Why on earth would Julie be texting me at six fifteen in the morning?

How was she not asleep right now?

In fact, how is *anyone* awake at this hour today?

I swiped up to read her text, my eyes adjusting to the bright display screen.

Did you get my autograph?

I rolled over in bed, groaning in response, though I knew she couldn't hear my disdain through the phone.

No, I texted back, throwing my phone on the pillow beside me before letting my hand fall over my eyes as my entire body tried to wake up.

I felt sluggish and tired, not at all like myself.

Probably because I tossed and turned all freaking night.

Though I was also harder than a slab

of marble at the moment. Instinctively, I let my free hand find its way in my boxers, if only to adjust myself for the moment. A nice shower session would take care of my morning wood, no doubt.

I grumbled and groaned, removing my hand from my eyes as I swung my legs over the side of the bed and stumbled to my bathroom.

The light was blinding to my eyes, as was my disheveled reflection in the mirror. I didn't waste time, removing my boxers quickly, my cock springing forth, free from its restraint.

Within seconds, I had the shower running and stood there waiting for the spray to heat up. The minute my feet hit the cool tile floor, I felt a wave of relief. I ran my hands through my hair, getting it wet first as I closed my eyes, letting the warm water sluice over my skin.

I reached out, bracing my palm against the tile as I let my free hand travel to my erection, the relief of my touch flooding me almost instantly. I let out a groan as I tightened my grip around my dick, slowly building a wet, warm rhythm.

My mind wandered like it always did, the familiar fantasies filling my brain. Fantasies I'd never share with anyone, because I had no one to share them with. It wasn't like I imagined an idol or a celebrity, or even one of the hot firemen that graced the calendar in my kitchen.

No, all I ever imagined was a man, a tall, dark, tattooed man, who was every bit the alpha type—large and in charge, cocky. I'm sure most people thought of such men, usually in the dominant role, owning them, making them beg for more. But in my fantasies, that big, strong, beautiful man got on his knees for *me.*

My cock throbbed as expected, clearly familiar with this song and dance. But my brain threw me for a loop, when the man I imagined staring up at me, licking his damn lips wasn't the generic, tall, dark and handsome I usually imagined, no.

Instead, I saw deep, mischievous green eyes, dark hair falling in them like shadows.

Tattooed hands perched palm flat against his tight, ripped jean-clad thighs, Drew Axel stared up at me like a devil, and I was powerless to push the thought aside.

Not when my cock throbbed, my fingers brushing over the burst of precum that had started to form at my head from the thought alone.

I was alone, in the privacy of my own home, so what did I have to be embarrassed about?

It wasn't like I was ever going to see the man again.

"I'll give you a fucking axe to grind," I grit out through my teeth, my hips picking up their pace as I thrust myself into my warm hand.

I knew it wouldn't be long from the tightening in my balls, the pulse of my cock as I imagined *shoving* my weeping cock in between those pouty, perfect lips of his. Just the thought of those lips wrapped around my cock, of his tongue along my shaft while I thrust myself into the back of his throat was enough to make me blow.

The muscles in my thighs and ass clenched as I squeezed myself, letting out a desperate moan as I opened my eyes. I came hard, and fast, my abdomen clenching as my body worked to dispel the culmination of my orgasm, watching as rope after rope circled the drain, taking with it my sanity and leaving a fresh wave of guilt in its presence.

It wasn't like I hadn't ever jacked off to the thought of a celebrity before, but this felt different, even though I couldn't explain why.

So instead of dissecting that, I decided

to just put all thoughts of hot Drew Axel fantasies out of my mind.

It's just fresh in your mind, that's all.

Doesn't mean you actually like the guy.

I told this to myself, I think because I wasn't ready to accept the truth, and that truth was that my life would never be the same now that Drew had shown up on his rock and roll horse like some ripped-jeans savior.

I tugged at my softening cock, the feeling of elation leaving my muscles feeling loose and like Jell-O. Using my thumb, I brushed the last drops of my release over the tip, noticing the warm water had started to run cold.

Shit, I better get a move on.

I don't want to be late!

And with that, I pushed aside all thoughts of good boys on their knees, of sexy rockstars, and of melodic voices away, choosing to focus on what I knew was true, and not fantasy.

And the truth was I, Taylor Meade, had a job to do, and that was the most important thing.

CHAPTER SIX

Drew

"FINALLY. I THOUGHT I was going to have to peel your ass off the barroom floor again tomorrow morning," Howler said as she looked up from her Rolling Stone magazine, her bare feet perched on top of the bus's steering wheel.

Gross.

"Get your feet off my baby," I said as I swatted at her ankles.

She only had the audacity to stick her

tongue out at me like a kid.

"She ain't your baby, D. She's the label's baby. Which technically makes her mine."

I grunted in disapproval as she brought her feet down, closing her magazine as she looked at me with a wary gaze.

"You're in a mood. What happened? You drink the worm from the tequila again?"

"No," I huffed as I collapsed on the couch.

"Just... being home is always... a thing, you know?" I said.

Helena stood in front of me, hands poised on her hips.

"I do know. I also know that I've been waiting for the last hour on you to get your ass back here so we can get cleaned up good in a proper hotel."

"I don't need a hotel, I have everything I need right here—" I gestured to the bus, the disarray of clothes and merch sprawled about between guitars.

Howler huffed a sigh of her own as she helmed the steering wheel.

The four rum and cokes I'd had weren't doing me any favors. Once upon a time, I could drink anyone under the table, but not anymore. And especially not after my year long detox from alcohol while I'd been under Rozen's roof.

The man was very strict about his diet, and therefore *your* diet was just as important.

Can't be banging a bag of toxins without getting poisoned, right?

"This isn't negotiable, Drew. Civilization beckons us," she said as she turned the bus on, and headed off toward the Paradise Hotel.

Growing up, the Paradise had always been this epitome of wealth and success, at least to most of the inhabitants here. To have your wedding there was like having it at the fucking Biltmore. It meant you were somebody *important*.

I'd always wanted to get married, and maybe when I was young, I could imagine myself walking down the aisle in the Paradise greenhouse in the courtyard, with some polo-wearing debonair Prince of Monaco-wannabe, but those dreams would never see the light of day. Because life had a different path for me, one that included rock shows, interviews, and bright, shiny lights.

And I was happy with what I'd built myself, what I'd built for my bandmates.

Wasn't I?

"Come on asshole, let's go," Howler said as she parked the bus.

"Do I have to?" I asked mournfully, staring up at the prestigiously lit mansion turned hotel from the privacy of my tour bus couch.

"The hotel is much more secure," Helena said, her voice steady.

DREW

I hadn't had a stalker encounter in years, but the levity of the truth hung in the air like sour apple jolly ranchers hang around after you've eaten them.

Sour, and still present.

"Fine," I lamented, hating that even in my hometown, I couldn't just... be.

"Jorge and Jager are already set up. They left right after the show. Everything is to your liking, and if you have any issues..."

"I know, I know, you'll take care of it," I grumbled as I got up.

Helena looked at me with a softness I didn't know she was capable of. "Right. I'll take care of it. You just do what you're good at," she said.

"What's that?" I asked as I opened the door, letting the crisp air in.

"Smile and be pretty, of course," she teased as she held open the door to the Paradise for me.

It wasn't anything I hadn't heard

before in the twenty years I'd been performing. Smile and be pretty.

My mind wandered to my brief moment in the john with Taylor. *It's just part of the job,* I had said, and there was a truth to that.

So why did it make me feel so... empty?

Howler waltzed up to the front desk, whizzing past me.

I slowly followed her stride and by the time I got to the front desk, she was already handing me keys.

"Thanks," I said as I took the plastic from her manicured fingers, the sheen of white plastic shimmering like a freshly waxed chest.

The crisp, bright white and grey with gold interior of the hotel wasn't quite as I remembered, though I'd only been in here once. On Prom night.

My mind wandered back to those memories. I'd gone with Giselle, my cover.

DREW

I'd really wanted to ask Brayden Lowell to prom, but I didn't have the guts. Though somehow, I'd ended up leaving with one of the other football players that night, holing away in a room his parents no doubt paid for. It was the night everything changed for me.

Because when Brayden told me to get on my knees and suck him off, I didn't have to be told twice.

Something in me clicked that night, and I just knew. That was what I was meant for; that was what I wanted.

For a pretty, suave man with more class than me to boss me the fuck around and let me be who I was, who I really was in the dark spaces I didn't share with anyone else.

But in the daytime, the sins of prom didn't exist, and I soon learned that it was better to keep my sexual preferences under lock and key, until I'd found the right person.

Someone who would be more than happy to tell the world they loved me, and not give a shit what other people thought.

I thought Rozen was that guy. For a little while anyway, but I knew now, Rozen only wanted a project. He didn't want *me*. He just wanted to mold me into everything I wasn't, everything that he wanted in a perfect partner, and when he couldn't do that...

He fucking cheated on me.

I brushed past Howler as I headed for the elevator.

"Good night, Drew!" she called as I hit the elevator buttons, relishing in how quickly the doors opened so I could escape the awful memories plaguing me at the moment.

God, I hope they stocked the bar in the room. I need a fucking drink.

Maybe this trip, this tour, was a bad idea.

I didn't waste time as I stumbled out of

the elevator, intent on finding my room as quickly as possible. The hallways were lit with an amber ambiance from the scones on the beige and white wallpapered walls, casting an eerie glow on the long hall, like something out of Stephen King movie.

When I finally found my room, relief rushed over me.

The bar was fully stocked, not just with alcohol, but with a basket full of snacks. Though upon further inspection, it looked to be all *health* snacks, aka the ones I'd been filling up on for the last year that Rozen had recommended I eat, which only made me sad and disappointed. Maybe Howler didn't get the memo, or maybe the lines crossed somewhere. Still, my stomach rumbled as it had been hours since I had anything substantial before the show.

I fiendishly grabbed the box of whole grain crackers, pouring myself about two fingers worth of whiskey.

Dinner of champions, of rockstars.

I kicked my boots off, sequestering my snacks and drink as I got on the bed. I tossed the box beside me as I took a long drink before setting the glass down on the pristine, glossy surface of the nightstand. The linens were soft, almost too soft, but it felt good. Pillowy, comfortable. I hated to admit Helena was right, it was better than the tour bus.

But even as nice and comfortable as everything was, it didn't make me feel the way I felt when I was curled up on my couch on the tour bus, writing songs no one would ever hear.

Mostly because no one wanted to hear power ballads anymore. Especially by someone like me.

Briefly, my mind wandered to thoughts of Giselle and Taylor. Giselle had always been comfortable. It wasn't a secret in school that her family was loaded, but unlike the other students I went to school with, she never acted like she came from money. In fact, she was the opposite. She never treated anyone like they were beneath her, and she was friends with practically everyone. And she never once made me feel inferior or bad about the fact I lived by the tracks, the part of Jasper Springs that was reserved for trailers and low-income housing.

That's why I always loved Giselle. She didn't see privilege the same way the other rich assholes in Jasper Springs High did.

Money never mattered to her, only character did.

I wondered if Taylor was the same way or not. Clearly his put together style suggested that he cared about appearances, and he was friends with Giselle, so I knew he must at least be an interesting, good guy.

Is this his scene?

Swanky hotels and mini bars full of

champagne?

My cock stiffened in my pants as I thought about him and his judgmental, dark blue eyes.

The way he'd locked eyes with me as I sang, I knew I had him. I'd done my job and rocked his world, in terms of music anyway.

I'd hoped I could have gotten to know him a bit more over drinks and catching up with Giselle, but instead he only seemed to be intent on ignoring me, as if I wasn't interesting enough to give the time of day.

Normally, I wouldn't care. I know I'm not everyone's cup of tea. But damn straight I know I am someone's shot of whiskey, and I'm fucking interesting.

I'm Drew Axel. I've had seven albums go platinum, and I've played sold out shows across the fucking world.

But Taylor didn't seem to give a shit about any of that.

Which was... refreshing, actually.

My mind wandered to that weird tension that had formed between us, as if we were waltzing some forbidden, unknown dance, waiting for the other to strike.

I knew it was a weak move, but I couldn't help myself that I checked him out. I'd been oogling the man all night, and it wasn't just because it was my job.

He was perfect. Tall, dirty blond, handsome and clean-cut, like a shiny new toy.

Taylor Swift's lyrics about being handsome and looking like a devil perked up in my psyche. I sighed, pulling my phone from my pocket as I queued up *Cruel Summer.*

The opening rifts reverberated in the open air as I took another sip of my drink, my cock twitching, needing attention.

Maybe that's what I needed. A good drink and a good nut.

I set my drink down, deciding perhaps that would cure all my ails.

A nice, hot knight in pretty polos to own me and take away the pain.

But the reality was that I was alone, surrounded by the comforts of a life I'd built, with no one to share my healthy Cheez-It knock offs with.

Shame fell over me as I let my cock spring out of my unzipped pants. I'd barely even thought about eye-fucking Taylor, or his perfect cock—which I'd noticed was visibly erect before he'd shoved it back in its cage. While I didn't like to assume any man was gay, I like to think as a non-straight man myself, my gaydar was pretty functional. It hadn't served me wrong the last twenty years.

"Fuck," I groaned as I slid my hand over my shaft, my thumb teasing the stud at my already swollen head.

The thought of his gaze as it held mine, while I strummed my guitar, or the way he'd blushed when he checked out *my dick*, made my desire spread like wildfire. I increased my pace, stroking haphazardly as I chased my elusive orgasm.

And in the space of my psyche, no doubt thanks to the drinks and my weird headspace of being back home, my fantasy took new flight.

I imagined myself right back in this hotel room, on my knees, my shirt unbuttoned, waiting for my punishments, like the dirty little brat I was.

I thought of Taylor in a fine tailored suit, staring down at me with that same intense gaze I'd seen earlier, his hand stroking his cock as he readied himself for me.

For me. It was all for me.

"Oh fuck!" I said as I came without warning, my cock pulsing. I forced my hand over the head, if only because I didn't want cum stains on my brand new shirt.

I fought to catch my breath as I rode out the euphoria of my orgasm, feeling a mix of shame, guilt, and remorse. And as I softened, I breathed a sigh of relief, and swore to myself I'd put all thoughts of Taylor and tonight out of my mind.

Tomorrow would be a better day.

I was sure of it.

CHAPTER SEVEN

Taylor

FINALLY, AFTER A morning full of nothing but issues—my floral tape not sticking, the flowers all looking a tad bit wilty, since apparently the power went out last night—not to mention, my iPad register not working correctly because of said power outage, I was in desperate need of a break.

I reached for my large iced coffee, which I'd barely had time to drink between answering the phone, trying to get my flowers to perk up, and working on a funeral arrangement, when my cell phone rang.

It was Julie calling, again.

I half-contemplated not answering, because I wasn't truly in the mood to deal with anyone who wasn't a paying customer. I still felt off after my restless night, and my guilty masturbation session this morning, and wasn't necessarily having the best day. But I knew if I ignored Julie, she'd only keep calling until I eventually picked up, so I figured it was best to get things over with.

"Yes, Jules," I said as I sat down in my office, swiveling in my pale blue office chair like a child with ADHD, sipping on their go juice.

"Oh my God, Tay, you will *never* guess what just happened!" She squealed, her voice pitching to a sound I was sure wasn't even human.

DREW

I held the phone from my ear.

"You met Drew Axel?" I drawled, my voice full of disdain and sarcasm.

"No! I wish, but..." She caught her breath as I took another sip of my drink. "Giselle just called me," she said between breaths. "Aaron proposed!"

Instantly, I sat up straighter in my chair. "What?" I asked in awe.

Honestly, I wasn't sure the man was ever going to propose. Giselle and Aaron had met in college nearly eight years ago. It seemed even though Giselle had made it more than evident she wanted to get married, Aaron didn't seem all that interested in marriage. He'd noted on more than one occasion, he was happy with how things were. They'd been living together for the last six years, both had good jobs, and seemed content to just... be. It was rather refreshing, actually. And in the last year or two, Giselle seemed to think that was enough, and had given up pushing the idea.

So to say I was surprised… was an understatement.

"She said yes, right?" I asked, panic overtaking me.

"Of course she said yes!" Julie nipped. "Why wouldn't she say yes? Aaron is a dreamboat! He's like, perfect husband material, plus they've been together since like, the dawn of time."

I rolled my eyes. "Eight years is not the dawn of time, Jules."

"Details, details. Did you not hear what I said? Giselle is getting *married*. As in, planning a wedding…" Julie enunciated rather well her wording of wedding.

And I knew what she was getting at before she said it, mostly because my own heart fluttered with the idea.

"Oh, I heard you," I said as I spun around in my chair.

"Which is why I'm calling you.

Obviously, as a good friend and bridesmaid—"

"Has she asked you already?" I said, sucking down my drink, if only to quell the panic building inside me.

"Well... no, but I know she's going to! Hell, Giselle and I have been friends since like, the third grade. I know her better than anyone," Julie touted.

"Still..."

"So, I'm doing her a favor while she calls all her relatives, gets the news out there... I'm scheduling some local appointments to help get the ball rolling with the planning. Because time is of the essence, as you know," Julie said matter of factly.

"Uh huh," I said as Julie continued.

"I know you are busy with the Anderson's funeral arrangements, but maybe you could squeeze a quick appointment in?"

"Of course, anything for a friend," I

said, my smile widening.

"When were you thinking?" I asked.

"Today," Julie squeaked.

Shut the front door!

"Today? It's like eleven thirty, Jules. What time were you thinking on such short notice?"

Julie chuckled nervously. "Well, she said she was free this afternoon around two, so…"

I looked around my messy floral studio, which looked like a bomb went off.

Booking a wedding would be ideal, but Giselle wasn't just a wedding. She was my friend, and while I would work my ass off to give her what she wanted, a part of me had to acknowledge that maybe I wasn't what she deserved.

Giselle's family was more than well off, and I knew her wedding would be a black tie affair. The kind of wedding worthy of Instagram hashtags and social influence.

I was just a little flower shop in Jasper

Springs, with barely enough equipment for a wedding of one hundred and fifty people, let alone one like what Giselle was probably to be a part of. I could have bet the farm their guest list would be over three hundred. At least.

I picked at the finish on my Ikea desk, which had started to peel after one year of installing it.

It was a long shot, right?

But maybe, just maybe it was the shot I needed to take.

Fake it till you make it, right?

"Yeah, yeah, two is fine," I said, forcing a smile as I watched a roll of tape roll off the counter, hitting the floor with a thud that echoed my anxiety.

Julie squealed once more.

"You are the best, Tay! Thank you so much! I promise you won't regret this!" she said, making kissy noises before hanging up and leaving me to marvel in my caffeine and anxiety alone, once more.

EVIE RILEY

What have I gotten myself into?

CHAPTER EIGHT

Drew

"IF YOU NEED me to come pick you up later, just text me," Helena said, her bright eyes rimmed in thick eyeliner staring at me over her lowered window like she was nothing more than a Soccer Mom dropping her kid off at school.

I slapped the roof of her rental, a silver Saturn, doing my best impersonation of a troubled youngster.

"Yes, Mom, I promise."

"Fuck you," she snapped, but I didn't miss the grin hiding beneath her sourpuss expression. "Sound check is around four fifteen. I need you to be at Darby's no later than quarter to four," she retorted, flipping me off.

I nodded. "Understood. Thanks for the ride."

Helena appraised me with a judgmental look. "Don't mention it."

It wasn't like I *needed* to be chauffeured around like Miss Daisy, I was perfectly capable of renting and driving a car myself, but my manager was, if anything, a control freak, and insisted on being around pretty much all the time except when I was performing, and a part of me actually did like having her around so much. If only because it meant I wasn't quite as alone as I often felt. I watched as she sped off, feeling a sense of relief.

How boring is my life when my best friend is my freaking manager?

DREW

Staring through the coffee shop window on the side of the street felt foreign to me. I rarely went anywhere in LA without a camera shoved in my face, so the fact I was able to just stand on the sidewalk by myself without security, without *worrying* that I'd be mobbed by fiendish paparazzi was nice.

I caught sight of Giselle sitting at a table inside, smiling while she played on her phone, and a part of me didn't want to disturb her. She looked so peaceful and content, her ponytail spilling over her shoulder, her perfect smile.

She was bright like a moonbeam, lighting up the night.

I slid my phone out, taking a picture, adding a note with the lyric as I often did when I was inspired.

The problem was, I couldn't finish a song, not since...

Since the breakup.

But if I was being a hundred percent

honest, I'd been stuck in the writer's block loop for longer than that.

I used to love writing songs, but the songs I wrote that I performed over and over with the band, they didn't feel like *me* anymore.

Rather they felt like a distant memory of a person I barely knew.

Sick Little Games, Ricochet Heart, and *Electric Sexxx* were great songs, but I was long past fucking around for the sheer fun of it. I wanted more.

But I wasn't able to define what that *more* really meant. Not at that moment anyway.

So, I decided to shove down my thoughts and put on a happy face, which wasn't so hard given the fact I was meeting up with an old friend—an old friend who had the unmistakable quality to light up a room no matter where she was.

"Morning, beautiful," I drawled as I

pulled up a chair across from her, popping her bright little bubble.

"Good Morning," she said, her smile huge.

"I hope you had a good time last night," I said.

Giselle nodded. "The best. But this morning..." Her grin widened, her eyes sparkled.

Before I could even ask, she thrust her hand in my face, and I would have had to be blind to miss the gigantic rock on her finger that was most certainly not there last night.

Sweet baby Jesus.

I gingerly took her hand, inspecting the specimen of a diamond that could only have come from a man with supreme taste and high standards.

"Congratulations," I said, mustering all the excitement I knew was needed for a moment such as this, but I'd be lying if I said it was genuine.

Not that I wasn't happy for her, but...

Giselle pulled her hand back, giving me a look.

"I'm sorry but this trumps *everything else*," she said poignantly.

"As it should," I responded, my tone much grumpier than I intended.

"I know it's sudden, but I'm already heading into planning mode," she said as she sipped her coffee.

"What have you been engaged for like, twenty minutes?" I teased.

Giselle smirked. "More like four hours." She giggled.

"You mean your future husband proposed to you at like, eight in the morning? Who does that?"

"Over breakfast before he left for work, yeah," she gushed.

I didn't want to begrudge her happiness like a Debbie Downer, but that didn't sound at all romantic to me. It sounded spontaneous, sure, but not romantic.

I'd always imagined if someone proposed to me—not that that would ever happen with my track record—it would be somewhere special.

Maybe in a castle or something in Scotland.

Or the Paradise at sunset.

"You guys been together long?" I asked, feeling slightly uncomfortable. Not because I wasn't happy for her, but because despite that, I still felt like *I* was the one who had gotten fucked over again.

Seeing folks legitimately enjoy one another, getting engaged, married even... it was like salt on a fresh wound when you were single and knew you'd probably never have those things.

Plenty of guys were interested in getting married, but the ones I'd met clearly weren't interested in marrying *me*.

"Yeah, eight years. We met in college, knew each other for a minute before we started dating about eight years ago." She beamed.

"Oh," was all I could muster, because I could feel the fear of missing out starting deep in the pit of my stomach again.

I needed to get my head out of the clouds and back on Earth. Focus on my music, the one thing that would never truly leave me alone.

"My friend, Julie, even made me an appointment with the florist. You should come with!" she said excitedly.

"I don't know about that. Don't you think you're jumping the gun at least a little bit?" I asked.

Giselle waved at me, dismissing my obvious disdain.

"Absolutely not. A woman can never be too prepared when it comes to wedding preparations. Unless of course, you have other plans..."

The way she said "other plans" hit me in the chest like a baseball bat.

I didn't have sound check until at least four, and the concert didn't start until nine.

Aside from our meetup, I hadn't really planned on doing much else other than mope around my fucking hotel room, doomscrolling, and trying to avoid anything and everything that had to do with Rozen, who was promoting his newest movie, some sci-fi alien thing I hadn't bothered to learn the name of when we'd been together.

With his new boy toy and co-star, nonetheless.

I shrugged.

Maybe getting out was what I really needed. To put myself outside my comfort zone and distract myself. Maybe it would even inspire me to write some more.

My heart melted a fraction. "I don't," I said.

And because I have the worst luck imaginable, that was the time Rozen came across the screen with my replacement project, Cedric Harlow, both men wearing fine suits, looking hot as hell on daytime television, yapping about said film.

"Fucking figures," I mumbled as I looked away.

Giselle glanced at the tv then at me, her eyes going wide. "Oh! I am so sorry, I didn't think... I mean, if you're anti-wedding, I wouldn't blame you if you didn't—"

"I'm not anti-wedding," I said with a sigh. "I just don't think it's in the cards for me, ya know? I haven't really had the best luck, haven't exactly met Mr. Right. Everyone I meet is Mr. Right Now, and being famous doesn't really sweeten the dating pool like you'd think."

It was actually quite the opposite. Everyone I had ever really been interested in, or thought about long-term seemed to only see me as a flash in the pan. Something to mess around with in hopes

I'd write a song about them and elevate them.

Kind of like a tattooed male version of Taylor Swift.

Giselle's gaze softened as she reached out for my hand. Her palm against the back of my hand was soft and warm, and damn if it didn't feel nice. It felt like old times, to be honest.

"Did you love him?" she asked genuinely.

"What?" I asked, shaking my head.

Seeing my ex, acting as if nothing had happened, as if I didn't even *exist* anymore...

It hurt.

Her question was expected though, honestly. Plenty of people asked that question, especially in the aftermath, personally at parties or even in interviews.

And I'd told everyone what they wanted to hear. I played my part. Mostly because Howler and the record execs had given me specific talking points I was not to deviate from. And I hadn't.

I'd played the scorned lover easily, because I was scorned.

Publicly humiliated on TMZ, no less, being thrown out of *our* home. The same home he still got to live in, with Cedric now in my place like the cookie cutter boyfriend he is. All sugar, no substance. Easily pliable for Rozen to mold into his dream boy.

"I don't know," I said honestly.

Giselle frowned.

"He... he was like this force that just pulled you in. Unrelenting, unstoppable. Made you feel like the center of the universe," I said as I squeezed her hand. "Until he decided on a new universe, that is."

"Cedric?" she asked, and I could tell even if she didn't want to admit it, she kept tabs on me. I wished I could say I was surprised.

DREW

"Yeah. Came home from a concert and found them in bed together," I said, worried I was divulging too much. But I trusted Giselle, even though I hadn't seen her in twenty years. I just knew my secrets would be safe with her. They always were.

And even though it'd been twenty years, she was still the same sweet, caring, warm woman I'd buried my secrets with long ago.

"I'm sorry, I didn't mean to be so insensitive," she said. "You don't have to talk about it if you don't want to."

"You're not being insensitive. Actually, I... I think a change of scenery might be good for me ya know?" I responded. "Surround yourself with positive things, and maybe you will start to attract positive things, right?"

She smiled at that.

Fake it till you make it, right?

CHAPTER NINE

Drew

AS WE WALKED up to the blue awning of *Taylor Made Bouquets*, I couldn't help but feel like maybe this trip was what I needed.

Normally, when I did shows with the band, we didn't stay in place long. As soon as one show was done, we'd be packed up and ready to go by the next morning. Between tours however, I relished being home.

Eating secret Doritos and catching up on Netflix when Rozen wasn't around.

But until he had very publicly thrown me out, I hadn't really given a thought to what home was.

For me, home was the road.

Or technically, now, it was my LA condo, which I only really visited a few times a year. I'd been traveling since I was fresh out of high school.

Being back *home* though, in Jasper Springs, where I grew up, made me realize that maybe that was what was missing in my life.

A real home. The kind of place people actually wrote songs about.

Just a small town boy, living in a lonely world.

Maybe after this trip I'd consider looking for an actual house. The kind with a wrap around porch made for lazy days where I could just sit on the deck and play my guitar while the damn sun went down.

Hell, maybe after all of this was said and done, maybe I'd even look for something in Jasper Springs, where people knew me, but where I was still left alone without a camera in my face twenty-four seven.

I opened the door for Giselle, my senses immediately hit with the onslaught of flowers.

The shop itself was nice, modern. It reminded me of some of the swanky boutiques in LA; all white and grey with sprinkles of pastels and jewel tones. I half-wondered if the ivy wall behind the counter that housed a bright neon sign that read "Good Vibes" in fancy script with a heart was actually real or not.

But my blood instantly ran cold the moment the owner of the shop came out of his office, sucking loudly on his straw from his iced coffee, wearing a pale blue button up that was rolled up to his elbows. His sandy hair hung in his pretty blue eyes that widened when they saw me.

Taylor *Made Bouquets.*

What were the fucking odds?

I guess pretty good when you lived in a town as small as Jasper Springs.

"I... didn't think you'd be bringing *him* with you," Taylor said as he blinked, instead focusing on Giselle who hugged him.

Giselle laughed. "When in Rome, right, Drew?" she said, flashing me a wink.

All I could do was nod because I was speechless. That we ended up in Taylor's shop, but also because...

Damn, he looks good all dressed up.

His pants hugged his ass nicely—I couldn't help but notice when he hugged Giselle—and he looked like he'd stepped out of a Calvin Klein ad back in the day. Timeless, attractive.

And my cock more than agreed,

despite his attitude.

In fact, if I was being honest, the attitude certainly helped.

Bad idea, Drew.

Bad, bad idea.

You just got out of a long public relationship.

You're supposed to be focusing on yourself!

"I suppose," he murmured, his gaze flashing to me before focusing back on Giselle again. "Congratulations," Taylor said as he held her hand in front of him, marveling at the bling on her finger.

"Thank you, and thank you for seeing me on such short notice," she said, tucking some hair behind her ear.

I slid my hands in my black jean pockets, taking that moment to waltz around the room so I could focus on anything other than the grade A specimen in tight khakis and a button down.

Fuuuuuck.

My cock twitched as I added that sight to my future spank bank.

Just the thought of popping those pretty pearly buttons on his shirt, at getting an eyeful of the bulge in those pants, was enough to make me feel more than engorged. I shifted my erection, trying to be as nonchalant as possible as the two of them chatted.

"Are you coming?" Taylor asked, the words going straight to my groin.

Fuck me sideways.

I cleared my throat as I turned my body halfway, so as not to draw attention to the massive erection in my pants that I'd sprung because of Tempting Taylor over there.

"Uh, yeah, of course," I said, probably a little too quickly.

Taylor narrowed his gaze, pursing his lips as if he knew.

Suspiciously aware that I didn't want to cum, I *needed to.*

"Okay, well, let's get on with it then," he said abruptly as he wrapped his arm around Giselle and corralled her into his office, leaving me and my damn hard on alone in the showroom feeling guilty as all hell.

The saccharine melody of my girl Taylor carried through the shop speakers like a whisper, lamenting my own thoughts about being enchanted to meet him.

She sang on about sparkling nights and not letting it go, and I had to take it as a sign.

So I sucked in a deep breath, tried to think unsexy thoughts, and followed the man of my literal dreams and my friend into the unknown.

CHAPTER TEN

Taylor

OF ALL THE people in the world, the last person I expected Giselle to bring into my shop was the rockstar.

I mean, we were just out last night, shouldn't he be off on his way to the next show or something?

After the morning I'd had, I was already all over the place, and a distraction—even a *hot* distraction—was bound to throw me off.

And I didn't want to fuck up the chance to land a job doing exactly what I opened my shop for.

Weddings.

I'd always been in love with the idea of being in love, I guess. Not to mention there was just something about the idea of walking down an aisle adorned with rose petals toward the man of your dreams, all dressed up in a fine suit... with the look on his face when he saw you...

So I'm a hopeless romantic. Sue me.

I watched as they both curled into their respective chairs. Giselle looked poised as always, like the quintessential bride-to-be; glowing, not a hair out of place, spine straight.

Drew, on the other hand...

He barely fit in my modern gold and velvet chair. He crossed his legs, resting his ankle on his knee as his larger frame spread out in the small space. The motion drew attention to his black jeans, and I had to look at the screen, if only to prevent myself from blushing as I remembered our awkward moment in the men's room the prior night.

Bad idea, Taylor.

Don't go down that road...

"Okay, so I'm thinking orchids and monstera, perhaps some exotic lilies..." I watched as Giselle's eyes widened in excitement.

"What about roses? Aren't roses your favorite flower?" Drew asked as he shifted his weight in the chair.

Giselle smiled, nodding. "I can't believe you remember that, but yeah..."

Drew shrugged. "How could I forget? You wore them to prom."

Giselle fell back in her chair with a giggle. "I did, didn't I?"

It was my turn to raise an eyebrow. Sitting next to one another they couldn't have been more different. Giselle and her perfect manicure, shiny, silky ponytail and her all around aesthetic against Drew in his black jeans, ripped tank, his arms lined with all those tattoos.

I swallowed harshly as my gaze traveled up his arms, over the intricate linework and the muscle. Even underneath all the ink, I could see the swell of his biceps, see the pronounced vein running through them. My cock jumped at the sight of his exposed hips, that delicious hip bone cutting my vision to where it certainly shouldn't be.

Focus, Taylor!

"Taylor?" Giselle pulled my wandering thoughts from the ether, and I realized at that moment I'd been staring.

At Drew and his large... presence.

I cleared my throat, shaking my head as I brought up some designs in the computer.

"Yes, well, I'm sure we can add some roses to the arrangement, if it is something the *bride* requests," I tutted as I shot Drew a scathing look. He only had the audacity to look offended, as if I had done something wrong. As if he wasn't offsetting the entire vibe of my workplace.

God he smells so good.

What is he wearing?

Just as I turned to address Giselle, I noticed Drew was staring.

At me.

Oh shit!

Do I have something on my face?

Did I spill my coffee on my shirt again?

"Take a picture Drew, it'll last longer," Giselle said coyly as she shoved him.

"What?" he responded, completely dumbfounded.

Perhaps I was wrong. Maybe he was just bored. After all, I couldn't fathom the drudgery of this town compared to everything he'd probably seen.

Hell, who was I kidding, what he probably saw on a daily basis.

"The flower arrangement..." she said with a twist of her lips as she pointed to the screen where I'd brought up a selection of arrangements.

"Yeah, uh, well, it's not *my* wedding, so..." he scoffed as he sat up straighter.

"I can email you the arrangements and you can look them over if you'd like. Take your time, get back to me if you have any questions," I said as I broke my impolite staring.

The man in black sitting in front of me almost sounded... sad.

Jealous, even.

But what on earth would Drew Axel be jealous of?

"Oh, that would be super!" Giselle said with a squeal as she rose from her seat. Drew grunted his opinion, and I nodded.

"I'll walk you out," I said as I rose from my chair, walking around my desk and skirting past the lumbering rockstar in my presence. But due to his size, not to mention the size of my office, there wasn't much space.

In fact, as I rounded my desk, my damn shoe caught the corner and upended me smack in the middle of Drew's lap.

Face first.

Directly against his...

Hardness.

Fucking hell!

I scrambled to my feet as heat rushed up my neck and into my cheeks.

"I'm so sorry," I said as I brushed myself off, even though I wasn't covered in anything but shame, and no amount of detergent would fix that.

Drew set his hands on my arms, steadying me as he rose, and I noticed how warm his palm felt against my exposed skin.

Giselle only laughed as she scooted past us.

"Don't mention it," Drew said with a

smirk.

I realized he hadn't let go of me, and I didn't hate it. In fact, I kind of liked how his palm felt against my skin. Warm. Friendly even.

I regrettably stepped away from his touch and slid past him to the door, following Giselle out.

When we'd gotten back in the shop workspace, Giselle regaled me with a hug and air kisses as she touted about her next shindig. I'd expected Drew to leave *with* her, but instead he just stood there, looking at all my display flowers, my chaotic space with shreds of tissue paper, floral blocks, and ribbons.

"Is there something else I can help *you* with, Mr. Axel?" I said poignantly as I crossed my arms. I really did need to get back to work, to email those files of arrangements off to Giselle like we'd discussed. I could have ignored Drew, but as I said—I was all over the place.

DREW

I noticed Drew was tapping his fingers on his thigh, quite rhythmically, mumbling something almost incoherent.

Ah, so he's certifiable too.

All the best musicians are, right?

"What?" He turned around, the light shining through the window on him like some Halo as the notes of *Teardrops On My Guitar* chimed over the speakers.

I forced a polite smile as I tried to focus on *anything* but him.

What the hell was he still doing here?

I took two steps forward, noting he didn't move. His bright green gaze settled on me as he continued to hum, and I realized he was singing.

He was *singing.*

I thought the performance of *Blank Space* was a one off, but he knew the words to one of the earliest songs of Taylor's career.

I slid my hands in my pockets as I stopped in front of him, raising an eyebrow.

"Didn't peg you for a Swiftie," I said, probably harsher than I meant to.

Drew shook off his weird aloofness, the motion making some dark hair fall in his dangerously dreamy eyes.

My gaze caught on the tattoos on his neck, noticing the black and white snake with red roses and a very flourished word I couldn't make out, crawling up his neck.

He licked his lips, running his fingers—also covered in black tattoos—over where my gaze hovered, and I noticed the *13* on his middle finger.

It's just a number.

It could mean anything.

The way his fingers moved over the expanse of his exposed skin caused my cock to twitch, and I murmured a slight curse under my breath.

Why was just that one touch so fucking hot?

God, I am a mess today!

"Didn't peg you for a florist," he said, flashing me a smirk.

"I've got to get back to work," I huffed, feeling quite on the spot, my own voice betraying me. "So, if you're not going to buy anything…"

"I don't think I can legally purchase what I want," he said with another aloof smile, one that reached his eyes.

I could feel the beginnings of sweat forming on my brow, and I knew I needed to end this—whatever *this* was before I lost all my marbles and dropped to my god damn knees for this man.

Which was *insane* because I barely knew him.

Maybe it's just the rockstar vibe.

Drew nodded behind me, at a small vase of cut pink and yellow roses.

"I'll take those, then," he said with a grin.

I huffed out a sigh, as this man was obviously intent on becoming the bane of my existence.

He'll be gone soon enough, and then you can forget him, his gothic gym-tan-laundry getup, and...

I grabbed the vase, practically sprinting to the counter to check him out.

"Fine," I bit as I set out to pack them up.

"Are you always this prickly?" Drew said as he leaned across the counter, the motion drawing attention to his exquisite arms.

I snapped the water vial on the stems, trying my damndest to focus, but it was hard.

And so was my unruly dick.

Now is not the time!

"Only around cocky rockstars who think they're God's gift to men," I said, realizing a split second later that I'd slipped up.

"And women," I hurriedly added.

I knew from Julie and her obsession

with the man and his band that Drew was tied to both men and women in the media, but I'd never paid much attention to tabloid gossip.

Drew laughed, and the sound was smooth. Like a double malt whiskey on ice.

"Noted," he said as I finished wrapping the flowers in their plastic, snapping the gumband in place as I rang him up.

"Thirty-five dollars," I said as I held my hand out.

Drew smiled and the sight was downright sinful as he removed his wallet from his back pocket, taking out a silver AmEx card.

No, not silver.

Platinum.

I ran the card with shaking hands, because at that point I wasn't sure if I was going to be able to hold my cool much longer. It was nearing three thirty and I needed to get the shop cleaned up and closed by four so I could work and get a head start on the Anderson arrangements in peace, and I was also erring perilously close to needing to rub one out in my damn office like a frustrated teenager.

What the hell is wrong with me?

I hurried through the motions, ripping off his receipt from the printer, and searching amidst my messy counter for a pen.

When I finally found the floral-taped, felt-rose pen, I passed it to him, and our fingers brushing for a moment, like in the movies.

Like in my dreams.

Like in a romance novel or something...

I pulled my hand back with haste as he jotted down his autograph, sliding the receipt back, his dark sapphire eyes staring at me like he was challenging me to a bar fight or something. I didn't miss how the heat in his challenging gaze made my cock throb, and it was all I could do to lean on the counter, my hardness pressing against the acrylic backing to try and stifle my god damned erection.

"Have a nice day," I said as I all but shoved the flowers across the counter to him before excusing myself to my office where I could lock the door.

Where I could escape the damn rockstar who was so far out of my league.

When the door chime rang, I let out a deep breath, and adjusted my cock before heading out to lock up the shop. Just as I flipped the lock, my phone rang. I turned around the corner, making a beeline for my office.

"Jules, now is seriously not the time," I nipped as I slumped down into my chair, trying to catch my breath.

"Oh, I'm sorry. Are you still with G? Is she there?"

I sighed as I unbuttoned my pants, if only because the strain against my unruly cock was starting to mar on the side of painful.

Think unsexy thoughts.

Think unsexy thoughts...

I tried to focus on my conversation, hoping that would be enough of a distraction.

"No, she just left a little bit ago, but it's been a chaotic day," I grumbled. "You'll never guess who she brought with her though." I sighed, running my hand over my face.

"I swear to all that is holy, Taylor, if you say she brought—"

"She did. She brought the rockstar."

Julie squealed again at a frequency I was sure would make a dog or cat deaf, as she clamored on with excitement. I pulled the phone away from my ear.

"Oh my God, Tay! I need all the details! Please tell me you got me an autograph..."

"I don't know, does his John Hancock on a receipt for flowers count?" I chirped.

My cock was still throbbing, twitching at the memory of him leaning across the counter, those delicious muscles...

Fucking hell.

I swallowed harshly as I brought my hand to my cock, adjusting myself once more, but it only served to be a nuisance as my cock sprang forth from the slit in my boxers like a damn Jack-In-The-Box.

"You are seriously the worst wingman, ever!" She huffed furiously. "At least tell me what he was wearing," she said.

My cock twitched again as my memory filled in the blanks.

This was a bad idea.

I squeezed my cock, taking a deep breath as I tried to combat my sudden horniness and focused instead on strategically answering Julie, who was waiting with bated breath.

"He was wearing black jeans, frayed at the knees, and studded boots. I couldn't tell the brand. They didn't *look* designer, but who the hell knows. I don't follow gothic fashion," I huffed as I closed my eyes, trying to catch my own breath.

"And he was wearing one of those awful muscle shirts like he was a rejected cast member from the Jersey Shore, which did nothing to hide his obviously tailored physique," I added with disdain.

Or the thick vein running up those biceps.

Christ, this was torture!

"But he was a total weirdo," I quickly added, needing to get my train of thought anywhere but on the thought of Drew Axel's exposed skin, his sexy muscles, or the those fucking tight pants and tattoos.

Or the way he ran his hand over his tattooed neck.

"How so?" Julie touted with surprise, as if this man she didn't even know could do no wrong.

"Well, for starters, he was lumbering around like a Deatheater in my salon, and then when we actually sat to discuss Giselle's concepts, he kept staring at me. And then I caught him humming Taylor Swift while he gaped at the salon after she'd left and—"

"Maybe he thinks you're cute, Tay." The pure joy in her voice was unmistakable.

My cock agreed with her notion, but I was not about to let that convince me of anything.

After all, I was... me.

I was the furthest thing from a spicy hookup.

I sighed as my thumb lazily stroked the head of my cock, feeling the wetness that had already started to bloom, cursing myself silently.

I huffed indignantly, if only to try and hurry the conversation along, but I didn't want to be rude.

"You read too many romance novels, Jules. I am not the least bit appealing to a man who has literally been with *the hottest man alive.*"

Julie sighed. "Sexiest Man Alive, actually. But in all honesty, Tay, you don't give yourself enough credit, you know that."

"I know," I said with heavy breath. "But I need to go, I have to—"

"Work, I know, I know," she said, before chiming in brightly with, "Oh! I should totally call Giselle and see if she and her new bestie are available! We should all hang out and get drinks! Celebrate!"

"That is a terrible idea," I growled.

Julie only had the audacity to laugh.

"Well, you owe me, Tay. That's *twice* I've asked you to hook a girl up, and you didn't deliver," she tutted.

I groaned, in part because she was right but also because the *need* to take care of myself was driving me up a fucking wall.

"Fine," I huffed, and then I hung up without warning.

I banged my forehead against my desktop, panicking because of what I knew I'd just agreed to. And as if fate had a better sense of humor than I did, I noticed that by doing so, the tab on my Internet browser had shifted to reveal an article I'd pulled up about the concert last night.

With an image of Drew on stage at M's Place, holding his guitar in between his legs, his bright eyes staring at me like he truly was challenging me.

Involuntarily, my hips thrust against my sweaty palm, needing the friction, needing the release.

I was so fucking hard, and he was so fucking *hot.*

So, I did the only thing I could think to do, despite knowing it was wrong on so many levels, and I'd sworn I wouldn't do it again. I leaned back in my chair, resting my head on the back as I stared up at the ceiling and closed my eyes.

I imagined those delicious muscles, the weight of his toned body on top of me, those tattooed fingers gripping my thighs as my cock filled his melodic little mouth. I imagined my fingers tangled in his sweaty, long locks as I shoved my dick to the back of his throat until I...

I came with a strangled grunt, once again hovering my hand over my head to collect my guilty release, my toes curling in my brown leather Sperry's as my orgasm ransacked me like a drunken concert goer in a damn moshpit.

"Fuck," I hissed, praying that by the sheer grace of God, Drew Axel would be out of Jasper Springs soon, so that I could get back to living my normal, boring, mundane life.

CHAPTER ELEVEN

Taylor

I'D JUST FINISHED wiping the counter around seven pm when I heard a rapping on my door. I'd fully intended on leaving the shop earlier, but halfway through cleaning I realized I hadn't done inventory yet, and thus, the work of a small-town entrepreneur never ceased.

But a part of me was glad for the distraction, to work off the boundless energy spurt I seemed to have fallen into ever since Drew Axel showed up. Not that I was complaining, I didn't mind a productive boost once in awhile, but this was different.

Because I knew if I let myself walk down Drew Axel lane, it wouldn't end well for me or my cock.

One look out the store windows and I immediately regretted *having* wall to wall windows in the front of my store, as it meant Julie was peering in with a look on her face that told me ignoring her would incite the apocalypse.

I sighed, throwing away the paper towel in my trash on the way to the door. I opened it to see Julie in all five foot four of her glory, her blonde hair perfectly highlighted and curled as if she'd recently been to the salon.

Dressed in a black form-fitting dress with a choker attached, her eyes rimmed in black smoky liner, she looked like she was either on her way to a showing of The

Craft or she had come here to sacrifice me for not getting her the autograph she asked for.

"The Satanic Cult is that way," I said dryly as I pointed to the left.

Julie rolled her eyes as she waltzed into my shop as if she owned the place.

I closed the door quietly and she apprehended me with a gaze that was practically Steve Harvey level judgmental.

"Don't tell me *that* is what you're wearing tonight?" She clicked her tongue against her teeth, her disdain more than evident.

I crossed my arms.

"I was not aware we were going anywhere," I said coldly.

Julie raised her eyebrow. "I told you I was going to call Giselle..."

My blood ran cold as I remembered what I'd stupidly agreed to in haste, because my feeble brain couldn't focus on anything but my need to sate my cock with a mind of its own.

"Yeah, but I assumed it was a no-go because you never called me back," I said as I headed back behind the counter to turn off the neon light.

"And give you enough of a chance to come up with fabricated bullshit about why staying at home is so much better? I don't think so," she said as she followed me.

I groaned in response. "Jules..."

"Nope, you're not getting out of this one, champ. You owe me," she said, pointing one long, coffin-shaped black nail at me.

Where the hell did she pull this look from? Eighth grade?

"And just where, pray tell, do I have to pay for my sins? And to what cost?" I narrowed my eyes on her.

She shrugged. "Drew Axel is playing tonight over at Darby's. Giselle suggested we all go, and hang out after."

DREW

I didn't miss the sparkle in her eyes at her words.

"Ah, so when I didn't bow to your request you pulled her strings, instead."

"What are well-connected, newly-engaged, and deliriously happy friends for?" she said, flashing me with a sly grin. "Besides, *I* did get her an appointment with the hottest florist in town. At the last minute."

It was my turn to cast her a look of doubt.

"I'm sure she would have come to the conclusion herself eventually," I said, but even I knew it probably wasn't true.

There were a hundred florists in the city, outside the realm of Jasper Springs that would be far better suited to the pedigree of Giselle and her no doubt, black tie, top of the line wedding.

Which reminded me just how badly I *needed* her business. While I didn't want my friend to feel like she *had* to choose me only because of our friendship, I wanted her to *want* me. I wanted her to see what I could do to make her dreams and her visions come true, and I wanted her to tell her friends.

But most of all, I just wanted her to look back on the beauty of her day and feel *happy*. I wanted to contribute to that happiness, because damn it I was a sucker for weddings and happy endings.

Like a lovesick sadist.

"There's no way out of this, is there?" I asked, pressing my lips together to stifle my burgeoning anxiety.

"Nope," she said, standing her ground.

I sighed as I grabbed my keys from the office. "Fine, but I need to stop home first, and shower." I was remiss to tell her the reason was because I'd busted a nut to her favorite rockstar in my office like a horny teenager.

I'd take that to my grave.

"Fine. But if you are one minute late

past nine o' clock..."

"You will feed me through the woodchipper. I know," I said as she rolled her eyes.

"Please, if I was going to murder you, I would choose something a lot less messy," she said with a grin, and I couldn't help but laugh.

I politely set my hand at her back, leading her out of the shop gently, and she relaxed against me, turning her face to stare up at me with pleading raccoon eyes.

"It's okay to have a little fun, you know," she whispered, even though there was no one within earshot who could hear us. The Christmas lights spread out through the trees on the sidewalk twinkled, casting an amber light against the setting sun.

I looked at her, feeling strangely seen. And perhaps it was because I'd had an off day, but I couldn't help but dispel my thoughts to the little witch.

"I know, but..."

"But what?"

We stopped as I approached her car.

"The last time I had fun, Jules..." I could feel my stomach twisting in knots as his name made its way on my tongue. I couldn't stop it.

"You know what happened... Zack happened. He was... in a band," I said breathlessly.

Julie's eyes widened, her mouth forming into a tight little o. "How long..."

I'd given the TLDR version to both her and Giselle, but I'd never told them about *why* Zack left me high and dry. To chase his musician dreams.

"Two years. High school. He left to pursue more *fun* things. And perhaps, more fun *people*."

Julie looked at me with sadness, and I hated it. Immediately, I regretted my words, running a hand through my hair.

"I think you're a lot of fun, when you're not overthinking," she said quietly. The crickets chirped, and the orange and gold clouds drew my attention.

"You have the prettiest voice," she said with a smile. "When you sing."

I rolled my eyes. "Everyone can karaoke, Jules. That's hardly a skill."

"Everyone can karaoke, Tay, but you can *sing.*" she said, flashing me a smirk.

"And you've got an amazing eye for art, you are one of the best shade throwers I know—"

"I do not throw shade," I said, letting out a laugh as I leaned against her car.

Julie fidgeted with her keys as she smiled back.

"You are the shadiest motherfucker I know," she said with a chuckle.

I sighed, feeling marginally better.

"All I'm saying is..." She sighed, before continuing. "It's okay to have fun, you know. I promise if you do I won't tell anyone," she said softly.

"I know," I said, feeling strangely emotional.

"Go home, get showered, get dressed, and be at Darby's no later than nine," she said, her tone changing to something much brighter than what she was wearing.

"Yes, sweetheart," I said, nodding in response.

Perhaps she was right.

Perhaps I did need to let loose, to have a little fun.

I watched her drive off before heading to my car, turning on the radio immediately. The beginning lyrics of *Style* graced my speakers.

And all at once the memories came flooding back.

Zack in his ripped jeans, practically bathed in sweat and beer from the night before. The night he'd stayed out all night.

Watching him throw his guitar into the

back of his pickup truck.

His words that cut me to the core.

Taylor Swift was blaring in my car as he looked at me, and I didn't even think to turn it off. The words about just asking someone to leave hitting me in my chest.

I'd stupidly thought he loved me.

The 'it's not you, Taylor, it's me,' speech. About how we were too different.

About how he couldn't breathe with me.

About how we just didn't work anymore, and he didn't want to be tied down to one dick forever.

About how he wanted more. Big lights, big cities, and crowds cheering his name.

He didn't want to hear me calling his name.

Not anymore.

I thought being together for a while meant we were a sure thing.

But I wasn't enough, and I'd never be enough.

Because I wasn't *fun.* I didn't like to get wasted at parties. I preferred curling up on the couch and watching romantic movies to staying up all night and being too blitzed to remember any of it.

I wanted a simple, romantic life of drinking coffee and doing the fucking crosswords together. I wanted to go wine tasting in Napa and spend my summers on the lake soaking up the sun with a man who made me feel like I was more than enough.

Like I was *his.*

I sighed, checking my clock.

Seven thirty.

Perhaps she was right.

Perhaps I did need to let loose, to have a little fun.

What was the worst that could happen?

CHAPTER TWELVE

Drew

"WHAT DO YOU want?" Howler said as she glared at me over her bouquet of roses.

"Can't I buy you flowers *just because*?" I said as I grabbed my amp, heading into Darby's.

"You can, but you don't," she said as she set them on the passenger seat of her rental.

"Well, let that be a memo to me to

shower you with flowers more often," I said as I kicked open the door to the restaurant.

"If you're going to buy my love, Axel, you should know by now I prefer booze and things that go buzz buzz."

I shot her a look, but I didn't miss the grin on her face.

"Buy your own sex toys, Howler. Your pussy is not my problem," I teased.

"That's not what I meant, and you know it. Fucking ass," she growled as she shouldered past me with the wheeled speakers.

After all, I'd bought her her last "buzz buzz." A custom green Ducati replica of the Green Ranger's Power Ranger bike when *Axe 2 Grind's* last album, *Sick Little Games* went Platinum.

I don't even have a custom Power Ranger bike!

Darby's wasn't necessarily a classy establishment, but it was definitely a leg up from M's Place.

True to form, my manager had everything delivered except me, my guitar, amp, and speakers. Helena might have been up my ass ninety-nine point nine percent of the time, but she was thorough, and the number one reason why my life ran on schedule.

The stage set up wasn't half bad either, and I didn't mind the open space.

M's was quite packed, but at least in this place I had room to move in the crowd.

I browsed my phone, waiting for Helena and the sound guys to finish setting up and fine-tuning their equipment so I could test my mic and guitar.

I propped myself on a stool, scrolling absentmindedly over Giselle's Facebook profile, which I'd added under my secret profile, AJ Andrews. I'd actually been born with the name Axel, because my parents were metal-heads, but very few people called me by my given name.

Axel James Andrews.

I'd garnered the nickname of 'Drews' my senior year because a substitute teacher accidentally read my last name as my first.

And the entire student body latched onto it, effectively erasing any existence of AJ Andrews.

When I'd signed with the record label pretty much out of high school, I'd undergone a "branding" initiative, basically a corporate record label makeover that turned me from AJ Andrews into front man Drew Axel.

Guess there was only room for one AJ in the biz, and that guy's been crooning hits since before I was born.

Howler had advised against any personal social media that wasn't tied to the brand, but all I really did on my profile was scroll for memes and periodically look up my classmates when I was drunk and depressed, so I wasn't sure what the big deal was.

I'd just come across a photograph of Giselle and a group of folks at what looked like Sunday Brunch, at a long table full of mimosas and croquettes and suddenly a pair of familiar blue eyes stared back at me. Taylor sat smirking in the corner of the photo like he knew I was checking him out.

Or rather his picture anyway, since clearly I'd proven to be a step above babbling earlier in his shop.

Real smooth, Drew.

I nonchalantly glanced up at Howler, who was berating one of the sound guys about wiring.

What crawled in her cornflakes this morning?

She'd been in a mood ever since we arrived.

Though I took the momentary break to

indulge myself as I hovered my finger over the names tagged in the photo. Julie Bartnett, Riley Evans, Giselle's brother Grayson, Aaron Evans, and...

Taylor Meade.

I'd clicked on his profile faster than I could blink, scrolling through his feed. There were plenty of photos of his floral arrangements—all striking, and beautiful, by the way—and Instagram posts from the shop, but not many of him.

Except the few photographs Julie and Giselle tagged him in. Brunch photos.

I scrolled past his feed until I hit what looked like an older image. Taylor was dressed in nothing but a pair of blue jeans and a white shirt, standing barefoot in front of a town home that looked like something out of a literal movie set. His sandy hair fell in his blue eyes and the smile on his face was the kind of smile you got right before you realized the world was fucked.

I recognized the smile, because I'd had it once too.

When I moved to LA, into my shitty little apartment while I jumped through the label's hoops.

The more I think about it now, the less I know, the caption said, with a lifetime event showing *Moved To Jasper Springs.*

I checked the date, noting it was posted seven years ago, which would make Taylor... twenty-five?

"Earth to Drew!" Howler barked as I was literally whacked in the head by a Koosh ball. The squeak it made as it hit my head only added to the insanity of the moment.

"What the fuck, Hel—"

"If you would have been paying attention instead of swiping right on your next rebound, you would have heard me say, *testing!*" she chastised as she crossed her arms.

I shut my phone off, sliding it back in

my pants pocket as I pushed all thoughts of Taylor and foolish innocence behind me.

It was clear that Taylor was a private person, and kept a low profile, and I knew that of all things meant I should stay away.

Let him live his perfect life in peace.

All I ever do is bring chaos wherever I go...

"Right." I slung my guitar strap over my shoulders, taking my stance in front of the microphone like I'd done so many times, and sucked in a deep breath.

Helena walked back to the back of the room, turning to give me a thumbs up.

I picked up my guitar. I didn't know why the first song that popped into my head was the song I'd heard in Taylor's shop but I went with it.

I sang about it being enchanting to meet, strumming the strings. The lyrics about wondering if they knew echoed in the space as I tickled the strings, closing my eyes and feeling the words as I always did when I sang a song by my favorite girl.

I covered the chorus once more, my voice echoing through the room, the guitar chords hitting deep in my belly. I opened my eyes to see Helena with her thumbs up, nodding vehemently.

"Sounds great, Drew! You should totally cover that one tonight!" she belted out through her microphone.

I continued to strum the melody, even though it was much more somber than what I usually liked to play.

"Okay, try something a little louder..." she ordered.

I strummed out some beginning chords of a darker progression, one of *Axe 2 Grind's* more recent hits—*Sick Little Games.*

"Tonight I'll be the monster and you can be my prey. Honey, I'll be the match, and you can be my flame..." I sang the words easily, my fingers dancing along the frets as I picked up the speed.

"Sounding good, baby! Now give me some screams!"

I rolled my eyes. She knew I didn't have any of my scream-o songs on the set list, but that didn't stop her from busting my balls once in a while.

I shook my head, playing right along, instead opting for one of her favorite songs, an MCR classic, *I'm Not Okay*.

"I'm not okaaaaaay," I screamed. I went on and screamed the next line too. And with a final strum of my guitar, I shot her a raised eyebrow.

Howler flipped me off, while touting into her microphone. "Drama Queen."

My phone vibrated in my pocket, pulling my attention as I held up my hand, making the cut motion to tell her to take five.

Giselle: Aren't you playing in Deer Park tonight?

Should I be concerned you've learned my tour locations? You're not going to turn into a stalker are you? I tapped back.

Giselle: Haha, you would be so lucky. No, I can promise you no stalking. My friend slash bridesmaid is a huge fan, and I thought maybe we could come see you play. You put on a hell of a show last night!

I eased up a little, though I shouldn't have been surprised that Giselle would want to bring her friend to meet me now that we'd hung out again. It wouldn't be the first friend of a friend...

Giselle: Taylor's coming too.

My eyebrows instantly rose as I thought about the little mouthy, khaki-wearing devil.

I'm performing at Darby's, nine o'clock. I tapped back instantly, punching the send button.

Giselle: Sweet! Maybe if you're not too busy being the hottest man alive, we can all get a drink. I think Taylor still owes you. She'd added flirty kiss emoji.

Oh Giselle, you haven't changed a fucking bit.

"Sometime today, Axel!" Helena called over her microphone.

Sure. I'll have my manager get you guys some backstage passes. It would be the last text I sent, because Helena pulled the phone right from my hands mid-text.

"Hey!" I nipped.

She raised an eyebrow at me, casting me her best expression of a dejected soccer mom.

"What or who is texting you?" she said as she started scrolling through my texts.

I sighed. Better to just tell her and get it over with, besides I did have a favor to ask.

"She's a friend, from high school," I said calmly.

Helena shot judgmental glares at me as she twisted her lips.

"So what, you're back to pussy now after one dick turned out to be a—"

"No, it's not like that. I promise," I said hurriedly, feeling quite queasy at the idea of Giselle in that way.

Gross.

"She's engaged," I rushed.

Helena cursed. "Jesus Christ, Axel. I get rebound but seriously, don't make me have to print out an NDA," she whined. "I *hate* printing out NDAs."

"They were at the concert last night, her and her friend, Taylor. He's a florist, and—" I sighed, knowing it was just best to be direct with Howler.

"I, uh... they're coming to the show tonight with another friend, and I thought maybe we could do like a backstage pass sort of thing for them."

Howler huffed as she handed me back my phone.

"So that's what this is about, huh? High School Musical wants the Drew Axel experience?"

"It could be worse," I nipped.

"How so?" Helena said as she pulled out her phone, no doubt sending off a text to whoever she needed to contact to get those passes to me as soon as possible.

"I could be out making a scene… getting drunk, flashing my junk all over the internet," I teased.

"If I ever have to scrub photographs of your dick from the Internet, you will buy me more than a new buzz buzz," she said, her tone quite clipped.

"I will buy you all the flowers, and a garage full of buzz buzz's, baby," I said, pouting for added effect.

"Done. Now get back to work. We have a show tonight!"

CHAPTER THIRTEEN

Taylor

"THIS PLACE IS pretty packed too," I said as I set our drinks on the high top.

We'd managed to get a table close to the front—again—despite my protests. Still, I was intent on actually *trying* to have fun with my girlfriends, even if that meant I needed a little liquid courage to do so.

Lord knows I won't be able to get through this show in one piece otherwise.

The girls had already started celebrating the occasion with a bottle of champagne, which was apparently compliments of the talent, as his *manager* had come by not even five minutes after we'd taken our seats, with a bottle and three glasses, as well as some lanyards with giant printed badges that read *GUEST*.

I'd barely gotten a protest out when Julie stepped on me, drawing all my attention to the sharp pain of a heel cutting through my Ralph Lauren leather shoes.

No doubt on purpose.

I dispensed the drinks—after we'd killed the champagne rather quickly. Just as I handed off Julie's vodka Redbull and Giselle's glass of pinot, the lights dimmed, and the crowd roared.

I hadn't spent much time in Deer Park, but the crowd the prior night certainly didn't hold a candle to the crowd at

DREW

Darby's. My gaze scattered the crowd, full of women like Giselle and Julie, who had also dragged their boyfriends and SO's—and probably some gay besties like myself—to this show, which should have made me feel less alone, but instead, it did the opposite.

I slid my hand in my jeans pocket, running the other one through my hair as I avoided watching Drew Axel coming on stage like the plague.

"How you doing out there tonight?" he called into his microphone, the crowd hollering in response.

Kill me now.

"My name is Drew Axel, some of you might already know me," he said, his voice lilting with charm that was smoother than melted chocolate.

Low, deep, sexy.

I grabbed my beer, if only to drown myself in it, when Julie literally grabbed me, practically squeezing the life out of me. Her movement forced me to turn around as she jumped up and down like a kid on Christmas, while Drew strummed his guitar, looking out into the crowd with a bright smile as everyone cheered.

"So... you guys want me to play some songs for you?"

Talk about edging, this guy is killing me.

"Okay, okay, well, let's start it off with one you *might* know. This one is called, *Sick Little Games.*"

Julie and Giselle both hooted and hollered as Drew's deep, gravely voice opened with, "Tonight, I'll be the monster and you can be my prey, honey. I'll be the match, and you can be my flame. Pour some gasoline on it, baby. Let's play some sick little games..."

Something about the way he held his guitar, the growl in his voice, and the literal way he actually *played*, his tattooed fingers sliding over the frets and strings, made my cock *ache*.

My gaze settled on said fingers, on the number 13 on his middle finger, the stars on his pointer and ring finger, the motion of his thumb.

The definition on his biceps as he held the beast of a guitar.

This was a bad idea.

This was a fucking terrible idea.

"Baby, you can run but you can't hide. I know you like the chase. I know you like the ride. So I'll hunt you down, baby. I'll show you how to slay, when you and I play our..."

The crowd chanted his words, the telltale sound like witchcraft.

Sick little games.

Baby, you can run but you can't hide. I know you like the chase. I know you like the ride.

I'd never been much for rock music, but something about the way Drew Axel *sang,* the way his voice turned dark and smooth when he closed his eyes, the way the lyrics sounded on his tongue... *fuck.*

The night prior, he'd performed mostly covers, and a few *Axe 2 Grind* songs, according to Giselle, but he hadn't played *this.*

I couldn't take my gaze off of him as he *shredded* his guitar, singing about playing sick little games.

And maybe it was the two glasses of champagne and a glass of beer, but both me and my cock found ourselves wondering just what kind of games Drew Axel liked to play.

"Tell me you want it while mascara runs down your face. Tell me you want to play sick little games," he crooned as the crowd went wild.

Including Julie and Giselle, who were now both practically screaming the lyrics.

It was hard to imagine the man on stage was the same man who'd been waltzing around my shop humming along to *Teardrops On My Guitar*.

And I think that was the moment I knew I was a fucking goner.

Because when he strummed his last note, he looked out into the crowd, and his gaze settled on me, as he sang, "Stay, stay, stay, so we can play our sick little games."

I took a long drink of my beer as I turned from his fiery gaze.

Its just a performance, Taylor, it doesn't mean anything.

Just like last night.

It's his job.

It's what he does.

The crowd roared as Giselle leaned in close to me, yelling in my ear as Drew strummed the opening notes of his next song.

"You okay?" she hollered into my ear.

"Are you gonna stay the night?" Drew sang in the background, his guitar roaring above the music from the speakers.

"Doesn't mean we're bound for life... so-oh-oh-oh-oh are you gonna stay the night?"

I pursed my lips, feeling warm all of a sudden as he sang a melodic, rocking cover of Paramore's song, *Stay The Night.*

I shouldn't have worn this fucking flannel.

I pulled at the collar, rolling my sleeves up to try and find some relief from the heat.

"I'm fine," I lied, but Giselle raised an eyebrow.

"I just can't believe you like... know this guy. Like *know* him," I said with disdain as I reached for my drink. "He's just so... so..."

"Magnetic?" Giselle said with a smile.

Not the word I would've chosen, but...

"I was going to say... edgy." I wrinkled my nose.

Giselle threw her head back and

laughed.

That was when I heard the crowd roar with excitement, the sound of Drew's singing getting louder, and louder.

"Oh my God," Julie squealed just as Giselle started pointing next to me.

I watched as Drew made his way through the crowd, from one side of the floor to us.

Making a beeline directly for *me*.

My blood chilled, and I froze, my beer halfway to my lips as his bright green eyes met my gaze. I could see the sweat on his brow, my gaze falling over his snake and roses tattoo. I still couldn't make the word out, but my gaze hovered there, just above his Adam's apple, along the pronounced thickness of the veins running up his neck, and underneath the skin of his sweat-slicked biceps.

Fuck, I was so hard.

And almost as if he *knew* the effect he had on me—on everyone, probably—he brushed past me, his thigh colliding with mine as he grabbed Julie, singing, "Are you gonna stay the night?"

But he didn't *look* at her.

He looked at me, and I didn't know how to feel about that, so instead I swallowed my beer and shifted my stance, trying to quell the second erection I'd sprung today for this devilish creature.

I watched as Julie followed him on stage, as he held her hand and crooned the rest of Paramore's song to her, telling her they weren't bound for life as he danced with her.

I watched as he spun her in a circle, knelt before her as he strummed his guitar, his gravelly, dark voice *pleading* with her.

And I watched her eyes sparkle, her smile widen like she'd just won the lottery. I wanted to be happy for her, after all he was her *favorite* rocker, and this experience probably beat out any autograph… but I was jealous.

Not that I'd ever been one to command attention. In fact, I was the last person who ever wanted to be lavished with attention in public. I hated being sung to on my birthday at a restaurant, and I never went out of my way to stand out—unless it was making TikToks for my business.

Maybe it was the alcohol.

Maybe it was the fact that despite my better judgment, this man did things to my cock, to my psyche, that I couldn't control.

Maybe it was because I was already halfway drunk, and perpetually single.

But I wished it was *me* on the stage, looking down at him on his knees.

I drained the rest of my beer, giving Julie and Axel my back as I leaned in to Giselle, yelling in her ear, "I need another drink."

CHAPTER FOURTEEN

Taylor

DREW GROWLED ON about being drunk in a car and crying like a baby into the microphone, belting out a rather heavy rendition of Taylor's *Cruel Summer,* the sound making my stomach flip.

He leaned forward, his dark, wet hair hanging in his eyes, the spotlights shining on the sweat that flung from his strands in the colored light as his voice crooned on about secrets.

I couldn't remember the last time I'd really been that level of drunk.

Probably after Zack left me.

Sometimes, I wondered what would have happened if I'd chased him.

If I'd had the guts to throw caution to the wind and go after him...

But when he left, as hurt as I was, there was also relief.

What kind of monster was *relieved* when someone left them for fortune and fame?

"Thank you!" Drew said as he finished, and the crowd collectively cheered.

"That was amazing!" Julie said as she hugged me too tightly for my own good.

Giselle drained the last bits of her wine, smiling wide.

"I think even *Taylor* had fun," she said with a wink.

I steadied Julie in my arms, wrapping mine around her waist so she wouldn't knock us both over. My legs only wobbled a bit.

"Yes, yes, I *did*," I said as Julie threw her arms around my neck with a giggle.

"I told you..." she said, her breath smelling of strong vodka.

"The fun isn't over yet," Giselle said as she pulled out her phone.

I turned to see Drew, who was bounding over to us from the stage. I could practically smell his sweat as he neared us, and I didn't hate it.

In fact, I kind of... liked it, if I was being honest.

Julie squealed with excitement as he stopped in front of us.

"You guys like the show?" he asked, running a hand through his wet locks, slicking his hair back.

Fuck yes, I liked it.

"You were amazing!" Giselle said with praise as Julie bounced up and down, still attached to me.

"I am like... your biggest fan," she said

with hearts in her eyes. Giselle laughed.

"Somehow, I doubt that, Jules," I said much harsher than I'd meant to.

Julie scowled at me as she removed an arm from my neck, smacking me in the chest.

Drew smiled a sly, devilish smile as he took a swig of the water bottle in his hand before nodding at us.

"You get my gift?" he asked.

"Yes, thank you!" Giselle said as she tapped away at her phone.

"We killed it before you even went on. After all, how else is anyone supposed to view your *show* without being intoxicated?" I bit out.

What the fuck?

Why did I say that?

Drew grunted a sound that went straight to my protesting cock, his tongue flicking out to slide over his lips.

"Taylor!" Julie scolded me.

Giselle didn't seem to notice, and if she

did, she didn't seem to care. Whoever she was texting was taking priority at the moment, and judging by the look of hearts in her eyes, I'd bet it was her now fiancé, Aaron.

"I am so sorry, Mr. Axel," Julie hurriedly rushed.

Drew shrugged. "It's okay... Julie, is it? It's like I always say, I know I'm not everyone's cup of tea," he said smoothly as he looked at me. "But I guarantee I'm someone's shot of whiskey." He flashed me a wink.

"Whiskey is horrible," I spat.

Drew only had the audacity to roll his eyes as he motioned for us to follow him.

"Come on kids, the real party's this way," he said, ignoring me.

I followed him and Julie, Giselle trailing behind us, through the back of Darbys into the parking lot, which was crawling with fans and security. On the way, Drew stopped to sign photos and take pictures, naturally.

Once we finally made it to the bus, his manager—Helen or something—met us at the front of the bus. Her piercing blue eyes looked us over like we were an alien experiment, scowling at us before regaling Drew with her disapproval.

"NDAs..." she said as she looked at him with fire in her eyes.

"Don't need 'em, Howler. These guys are *friends*."

Friends.

I certainly didn't see myself as Drew Axel's friend by any means. Acquaintance was stretching it.

"I'm holding you to that." She hushed as she turned to us, pretending she hadn't just scolded a grown man like a child in front of his *friends*.

How dare she talk to him like that!

I followed everyone onto the tour bus, surprised at how *big* it actually was. I'd always seen these things on television, and thought they looked huge, and I was right. Though it wasn't nearly as messy as I expected it to be.

Drew dropped his guitar off on the couch, waltzing up to the kitchen... er... bar as he grabbed four glasses.

"Who's drinking?" he asked as he went straight for the whiskey.

"Me!" Julie bounced.

Giselle nodded her head. "Does the day end in y?" Giselle said as she walked past me, joining Julie.

I ran my fingertips along the soft micro-suede couch, feeling on the edge of a precipice. My words betrayed me as I caught Drew's gaze, his eyebrow raised.

"Fine, peer pressure and all," I muttered, straightening my stance and blowing some stray hair out of my eyes. I was *hot.* "But I want something *harder* than whiskey. Lord knows, I won't be able to make it through this drudgery without something to knock me on my fucking ass."

Julie and Giselle giggled, but Drew only smiled.

"Noted. Taylor likes it *hard.*"

***

I didn't know what time it was.

I barely knew *where* I was.

All I knew was I was having the literal time of my life.

"Come on, Tay, just one song..." Julie pleaded as Giselle giggled, her head in Drew's lap as he ran his fingers through her hair like he truly wasn't some famous rockstar. Like he was just some guy she hung out with all the time.

Like he was her best friend.

I rolled my eyes. Drew raised an eyebrow at me.

"It's okay baby, we all know who the talent is here, anyway," he said with a smirk.

His words started a fire within me.

DREW

Was he... challenging me?

Was he... flirting with me?

I was too drunk to process either, and too drunk to say no.

"Fine, if it will shut you up," I said, as Julie screamed, "Yes! "

CHAPTER FIFTEEN

Drew

GISELLE PLAYED ON her phone, her head in my lap keeping me warm as I trailed my fingers through her hair, wishing she was someone else.

In a lot of ways, it was like we'd never left high school. Like the two of us were just back twenty years ago, trading Louboutins for Chuck Taylors, and football players for hot florists.

I couldn't remember when Taylor lost

his flannel, but I didn't miss it. He looked hot as hell in his tight-fitting, white tee shirt, dark blue jeans, and socks, his sandy hair taking on a sheen of sweat from all the drinking, dancing, and laughing.

I was no stranger to liquid courage. Lord knew I'd been in enough situations to require my own. But the moment he grabbed the karaoke microphone, something in him... shifted.

I barely had time to register the beginning notes as he closed his eyes. He opened them, staring right at me as he swayed his hips, grasping the microphone tightly, his bright blue gaze fixing me to my spot on the couch.

He drawled out the Taylor Swift song, going on about compliments and getting drunk and making fun, his voice something between smoky and seductive.

He closed his eyes, singing about a magnetic field being too strong, moving his hips and hands in that flourished, dramatic, over-confident way alcohol makes you move.

My blood ran cold, as the words about a boyfriend caused my stomach to flip.

I shifted Giselle in my lap, if only because my cock decided that was the moment to voice his opinion of Taylor's Taylor Swift Karaoke.

His pitch and tone was absolutely fucking perfect as he belted out the lyrics.

So the florist has some pipes.

I sang the next line about looking at his face, of my own volition, completely possessed by the moment.

By *him.*

Taylor returned with the next lines about being so furious and the way it made them feel, running a hand through his sweaty, dirty blonde hair, his sapphire eyes burning with intoxication, his words hazy and sexy.

Julie hollered, cheering him on.

Giselle shifted into a seated position, turning to look at me. I could see her out of my peripheral vision, but nothing mattered.

Nothing mattered except the most perfect man I'd ever seen in my goddamn life, singing his heart out for me.

The embers of my heart caught, igniting back to life what I thought could never be revived.

The embers of my heart...

The potential lyrics dissipated in the air as I moved forward, leaning my arm over my knees, pulled into his performance.

Ignited.

Captivated, I murmured the following line about them being gorgeous as he sang the words.

When the song was over, Taylor took a bow and threw the microphone back to Julie as he stumbled toward my bathroom, shutting the door. I wanted to go after him, to check on him, but Howler stepped in front of me.

"Jesus Christ, Axel, you know this isn't a high school party right?" she said with disdain.

I sighed, running a hand through my hair. "I know, Helena, I—"

"We should get going, Giselle said as she attempted to stand, but stumbled back to the couch with a giggle. I turned to look at Howler, who sighed, pulling at the skin underneath her eyes.

"Can you—"

"Yes, pain in my fucking ass, I can get the High School Musical Cast a damn hotel room," she nipped as she leaned down to help Giselle up.

"Come on, Jules, I think that's our cue..." Giselle said between a fit of giggles with a grin.

"Awwwww, but I'm not—"

"Come on, Scream Queen, that means you too..." Howler said as she literally corralled the girls like sheep, which was saying something given the fact she was smaller than both of them. Like a gothic sheepherder.

Cute, drunk sheep.

Make all the stable sheep go baa!

Laughter erupted from my chest uncontrollably as I imagined Howler in a long black robe corralling sheep. Howler shot me a look I can only describe as annoyed, realizing that I was laughing at my own jokes, my own internal monologue like some lunatic.

"We'll talk about this in the morning," she said pointedly as she led the girls off the bus.

"Does this mean I owe you a new buzzzzzzz buzzzzzzz," I said, my z's running away with me.

"Fuck you, Axel!" she barked, flipping me off as the doors shut.

I found my way back to the karaoke machine, the remainder of Julie's song finishing its last notes. I shut the system off, removing my shirt as I surveyed my bus. It wasn't completely trashed like it had been in the old days when I toured, but it was definitely a mess.

I collected the glasses, setting them in the sink, heading back to the main drag, when the bathroom door opened, nearly taking me out. I stumbled, as did Taylor, and due to the mess, both of us ended up crashing against the couch. I braced my arms around him, shifting my weight to cushion his fall.

His body was heavy against mine, and...

Fuck... is that...

"That a microphone in your pocket, Taylor or you just happy to see me?" I teased, flicking out my tongue to moisten my dry lips.

Taylor grunted an annoyed sound, but did not move otherwise, certainly not as I expected him to.

The feel of his hard cock against mine had me gasping for breath as my gaze fell to his lips.

"Shut up," he said, his gaze dark and full of heat as his hips *thrust* against mine, eliciting another deep groan from me.

I was acutely aware of the hazy blur surrounding this pretty little devil, just as I was acutely aware of all the blood in my body rushing to one focal point, a hazardous sign pointing directly to the man above me.

"Excuse me," I said as I breathed a shaky breath, rocking my own hips against him, my hand slowly sliding against the small of his back, against his soaked shirt.

His sweat was warm against my palm, and my heart was racing. My gaze flashed to his pristine blue eyes, waiting for encouragement.

Permission.

DREW

Taylor squirmed on top of me, his hands grasping the couch cushion to ground himself.

To keep him upright.

"I said, shut your pretty little mouth," he said.

I was aware the line we balanced was thin, but I was drunk, and so was he.

So I didn't think twice about pushing his obvious buttons.

I always was a sucker for a man on top.

"Make me, Taylor," I growled, sliding my hands into the waistband of his jeans, feeling his warm skin flush with mine.

I expected him to make some quip, but instead he *crushed* his lips against mine in a fashion that made me wonder if he'd leave a bruise.

But my entire body reacted like a livewire to his touch, my cock twitching, straining against my jeans at the feral heat of his tongue in my mouth, of his teeth biting my bottom lip.

"Fuck..." I whispered into his mouth, his hands finding their way into my hair, gripping my locks.

I scooted back on the couch, pulling him with me haphazardly, knocking my guitar onto the floor with a thud, my hands pulling at his wet shirt. Taylor leaned back to remove it, shaking his head, sweat dripping onto my lips from his movement. I licked the spot, tasting the saltiness, which only made my cock *throb.*

"Fucking hell..." he swore, the curse on his tongue a sound that was both hot as hell, and indicative of the alcohol in both our systems.

My gaze roved over him, now shirtless, his perfectly golden skin glittering in the light, down to the rather noticeable tent he was pitching in his jeans.

Fuuuuuuuck, I want that.

He must've caught my gaze, because

he smirked, looking down at me as he grabbed himself, his lips still swollen from kissing me.

"Is this what you want?" he asked, his tone dark and inviting. I grabbed myself, if only because I needed to be touched.

I needed the relief...

But my touch wasn't enough.

"Yes," I said hurriedly, watching as Taylor ambled backward, stumbling a bit but making his stance on two legs as he stood in front of me. I watched his fingers fumble with the buttons of his jeans, his fingernail catching.

I rose from my couch, closing the gap between us as I reached out a shaky hand, shoving his away. I settled one hand around his hip, holding him in place as the other flicked the button open, my gaze never leaving his.

I didn't miss the shaky breath that left him, or the way his cock twitched when my palm brushed over his denim trapped mound.

Fire blazed in Taylor's eyes as I slowly pulled on his zipper, sliding my hand between the waistband of his boxers and jeans, over the smooth surface of his ass, pushing them down around his ankles. His fiery gaze met mine, his swollen lips trembling as he stood his ground.

"Then get on your fucking knees," he breathed, his words settling on me like a steel beam.

"Yes, sir," I breathed as I stumbled to my knees, the animal inside of me ready to obey his command.

CHAPTER SIXTEEN

Taylor

MY HEAD WAS spinning, and I was certain it wasn't just because I was wasted off my ass.

I took a deep breath, my heart thudding in my chest so loudly I wondered if Drew could hear it.

I closed my eyes as his hot breath kissed my sensitive flesh, his fingers wrapping around my shaft as he licked me from throbbing head to base before taking me into the back of his throat in one fell swoop.

"Fuck..." I cursed, my voice full of desperation as he rolled his tongue around me, sucking with a tension that was so warm, so tight, and so good...

I feared I might blow my load right there.

I opened my eyes, my vision still a little blurry, but when I looked at Drew it seemed to sharpen.

Instinctively, I grabbed him by the back of his hair, my fingers tangling in his locks as I held him in place.

It had been so long since *anyone* had sucked my dick, and I was drunk.

The desperate sound escaped my mouth as I came without warning.

My knees ready to buckle, I thrust myself into Drew's mouth, riding out the waves of my orgasm like a merry-go-round.

I focused on the way Drew looked up

at me, his eyeliner smudged at the corners of his eyes. His fingernails dug into the flesh of my ass as I watched him swallow me down, his gaze never leaving mine.

When he pulled away, my heart beating inside my chest, I attempted to speak.

"Get up," I said, palming my cock as I brushed away any remains of saliva and cum.

Drew met my gaze, his smudged-mascara around his green eyes doing a number on me.

Fuck, he was so damn pretty.

He slowly stood, and I moved toward him, backing him against the couch.

I could barely speak, my brain and body coming apart at the seams. So, I spoke in the only way that seemed like a viable option at the moment. I pressed my lips to his.

Drew stumbled backward onto the

couch, pulling me with him, his tongue lavishing mine. I could taste myself on his tongue, and I didn't hate it.

I didn't hate it at all.

I slid my hands over his chest, finding his belt buckle as I groaned into his mouth.

My fingers fumbled with his pants, and from our proximity on the couch, I was only really able to get his pants down halfway to his knees.

I watched hazily as his cock bobbed free. The light glistened off his steel piercings, and my softening cock was already protesting being spent.

"Fuck, that's hot," I murmured as I worked my lips over his neck, over his snake tattoo, while my fingers played with his stiff nipple.

"Taylor..." His voice was all screwed up, the steel of his piercings cool against my warm skin as he thrust his wet, weeping cock against my abdomen, seeking the friction. I let my free hand wander slowly down his chest before settling at the base of his cock, taking it in my hand as my thumb ran over the piercings, one by one.

"I can't... I don't know how much longer I can—"

I sucked his nipple into my mouth, nipping at the sensitive peak, and Drew practically arched right off the couch.

"Fuck, fuck, fuck..." he cursed, thrusting himself against my belly with haste.

Despite the alcohol in my system, it seemed my cock had not gotten the memo. I removed my hand from his dick momentarily, grinding my surprise hardness against his, feeling the sting of the cold metal of his Jacob's Ladder against my sensitive shaft, trailing over the opening of my slit.

The sensation of his cock against mine, mixed with the heat and the metal was driving me crazy. I laved my tongue around his nipple, grinding myself against him as my thighs tightened, as I chased my own release.

"Fuck, Taylor..." He groaned.

I wasn't far off, and I could tell he wasn't either.

"That's it, come for me," I commanded, my voice not my own.

Drew intertwined his leg with mine, pulling me closer, and I couldn't hold off any more. I came again, covering his cock with my release, a litany of curses and his name leaving my lips even as he growled in desperation. His cock pulsed against mine, wet, warm spend slicking my abdomen, mixing together with mine as he let out a string of curses amidst my name.

I shut him up with fervor as I swallowed his moans, his growls, and his ecstasy.

Mine, mine, mine.

DREW

Drew collapsed against the couch, and I against him as the alcohol hit its peak along with exhaustion.

I laid my head against his warm chest, listening to the sound of his beating heart until slumber befell us both.

CHAPTER SEVENTEEN

Taylor

MY HEAD WAS *killing* me, and my stomach roiled like I'd ridden a rollercoaster one too many times, but that was nothing compared to the weight holding me down, pressing against my sore, tired muscles.

I opened my eyes, and panic immediately flooded my body as I found the source of said weight.

Drew fucking Axel laying on top of me,

mostly naked, his perfect ass in the air.

His pants were still halfway attached around his knees, and I was...

Also naked.

One hundred percent naked.

Panic and anxiety swelled within me along with the sourness of all the alcohol I'd consumed, and I didn't think twice about scrambling out from beneath him, and making a sprint to the damn bathroom. I barely closed the door before the urge to spill my guts hit me, my head throbbing as reality compounded my psyche.

Holy hell...

I leaned my head against the toilet seat, the coolness a stark contrast to the heat I felt as I tried to process what happened. What I could remember, anyway.

And what I remembered was for the first time in years I had... fun.

A little too much fun, and we...

DREW

The bathroom door swung open, and I turned slightly to look up at Drew, now dressed with his pants around his waist like a normal person, but still shirtless. I could finally see the majority of his tattoos. Both his arms were covered in intricate sleeves, and I could finally read what was covered before.

Reputation.

The snake that curled around the letters, with its bright red roses was written in the same vintage style text as Taylor Swift's phenomenal album art.

Big reputation, all right...

"You good?" he asked calmly, staring at my naked ass curled around his toilet. The guilt and shame mixed with strange feelings I wasn't sure how to process.

Like the part of me that *liked* the way he was looking at me right now, even though I was certain I looked an absolute mess.

I caught my breath as the nausea

passed, my head still throbbing.

"Yeah, I'm just peachy keen over here," I grumbled as I stood up, flushing the toilet, feeling more than vulnerable standing in Drew Axel's bathroom, naked as the day I was born. His gaze met mine, softening as he leaned against the door.

"Listen, Taylor..."

Oh no, I wasn't doing this. I was not about to do the awkward morning after thing with this man. *I never do this sort of thing,* I wanted to say, but what came out of my mouth instead was, "I can't believe I, that we..." I mumbled as the memories came crawling back

Of his tongue in my mouth.

Of his sinful mouth wrapped around my cock.

I didn't miss the way his shoulders fell as I brushed past him, needing to move, to find my...

Where the fuck are my pants?

Drew sighed. "If memory serves me

correctly, *we* didn't get that far," he said, flashing me a smirk. "Though the experience was more than satisfying, at least for me," he said shakily, his stare making my body heat.

I stopped to meet his green eyed gaze as the reality of his words covered me in truth.

It was all a blur of steel piercings, of warm tongues, soft hair and hard abs. I covered my abdomen with my hand, feeling the dried evidence of just how satisfied he'd been, like armor on my skin.

The memory of my own satisfaction, and the shame of just how fast Drew's expert mouth had brought me to release, surged through my brain, causing my stomach to flip all over again.

Panic laced through me as I recalled just how long it'd been since I'd been with *anyone.*

Seven fucking years.

After Zack had left, I hadn't had the heart to even look at another man, and over the years, any attempt to even try and work my way out of the shell I'd built just ended up disappointing me in the end.

I didn't *know* Drew Axel, not really. I didn't know anything about him except that being in the same room with him drove me crazy, that he was apparently a closet Swiftie, and he and Giselle had apparently grown up together. But I had no idea what his favorite food was, or if he preferred coffee to tea, or if the rumors about him and his long list of ex-lovers was true, and if it was...

That was a lot of pussy and dick the man had seen.

My entire body tensed as I wondered about the sexual health of a man who'd been linked to at least twenty people in the media.

"I don't even know if you're—"

DREW

Drew crossed his arms as he watched me pull blankets, toss pillows, looking for my clothes.

"Clean as a whistle," he drawled, his tone solid, smooth, but a little... sad? "I'm assuming you are..."

I huffed as I shot him a pointed glare.

The audacity of this man...

"If you must know, I've only been with one man in my short twenty-five years of life, thank you very much, so yes, I am sparkling," I nipped. "Where the fuck are my clothes?" I bit, feeling more than flustered.

Drew tossed my *fucking underwear* and pants at me.

"Well, I'm glad we cleared that up," he said.

Finally, I found my shirt practically buried in between the cushions, and I pulled it out.

I glared at him as I dressed myself.

"Where are the girls?" I asked bitterly.

"In the hotel. I had Howler get them—and you—a room, but, uh... obviously you crashed here."

I zipped my pants, angry that despite everything going on at the moment my cock was already semi-hard, just from the sight of this man standing around in nothing but a pair of jeans, looking every bit the bad boy rockstar he clearly was.

"Just another day in the life of Drew Axel, right?"

Dark hair hung in his face, tattoos on display, and sad green eyes with streaks of mascara smudged around the corners.

Now is not the time!

You need to get your shit together and get home where you can freak out and process all of this, and get back to your normal, mundane life!

I hopped into my shoes, ran a hand through my hair. Standing tall, I took one look at the sinful man in front of me, my heart twitching in my chest as a strange feeling of *longing* tugged at its strings. As much as I didn't want to admit it, I didn't *want* to leave. But I was a realist, and I knew one drunk blowjob did not equate to anything substantial.

"Taylor..." He sighed.

This... it was a mistake, and it would never happen again, because Drew would be leaving on his giant tour bus, off to perform in some other town and suck some other asshole off with his sinful mouth, right?

"Thank you for your hospitality, but I think I've overstayed my welcome," I mumbled as I shouldered past him, all but running off the damn bus.

Drew did not chase me.

Instead, he let me storm my way off, onto the pavement before he called out, "I think you forgot something."

My dignity?

My morals?

Perhaps my fucking brain...

I turned to see him slowly sauntering off the bus, wearing a loose muscle tank that I wasn't entirely sure was clean, and waving my phone in the air like a beacon.

Of course, how could I have been so stupid...

He stopped in front of me, the rays of the morning sun lighting him up like some sort of dark angel.

I didn't want to look at him, but I couldn't help myself.

"I think this belongs to you," he said softly, licking his lips as he held the phone out for me to take.

I reached out to take it from him, my fingers brushing his knuckles as I did so, and I noticed on his left hand, his knuckles were tattooed with the number 1989, with a heart on his pinky finger. My thumb brushed the smooth skin, the tattooed *1* slowly as my breath caught in my throat.

What the hell was wrong with me?

"Thanks," I said, swallowing harshly.

"It's early, Taylor. The girls are probably still sleeping," he said quietly, even though there was no one in the parking lot but us and a few cars.

His tone settled something inside of me, for a moment.

I pulled the phone from his hand, sliding it into my back pocket.

"I know you need to go, but... not on an empty stomach. At least..." He sighed, running his hand through his hair, the motion undeniably sexy as the sun lit him up. "At least let me buy you breakfast," he pleaded. "Soak up some of that alcohol."

My stomach decided to protest at that moment, giving me away.

My head still throbbed, and I was starving.

"Let me take care of you, and then... then you can grab the girls and leave, and I won't stop you," he said, his voice full of sadness that pulled at my hardened,

bitter heart.
    How could I say no?

CHAPTER EIGHTEEN

Drew

TAYLOR'S INSINUATIONS COULDN'T have been further from the truth, but I guess I couldn't blame him for thinking such things. It wasn't like my public image helped matters, when I was constantly photographed at parties, or leaving said parties in LA mansions.

The truth was, I wasn't the playboy the tabloids made me out to be. I'd never really put a label on my sexuality, which only fed into the public's assumptions that I was some hard-edged fuckboy who would put his dick in anything with a pulse.

But in reality, I was a one-man kind of man. I *never* took men back to my bus. Even when I was young and touring with the band, when they were constantly bringing girls back to party as I had last night, I never did.

Because stupidly, I just wanted someone to myself. Someone who wouldn't give a shit about my celebrity status and just wanted to fucking sing some karaoke.

Walking through the Paradise with Taylor was a surreal experience. As a teen with a dream, outside of Prom I'd never been capable of walking into the Paradise, because the price tag that came with anything in there was more than I could even dream of.

But walking in there with Taylor, the

both of us looking the furthest from *elegant* at the moment, was enough to make my stupid heart skip a beat. I imagined Taylor in his normal preppy attire—those tight fitting khakis, rolled button ups, hair slicked back—and I could see him perfectly there, sipping a mimosa.

But there was something insanely hot about his disheveled hair, his flannel rolled up to show his toned arms, and his perfect ass in those dark wash jeans, sitting at the table drinking a steaming cup of coffee, which I'd watched him put two sugars and a boatload of cream in.

"You didn't have to do this," he grumbled as he looked up from his menu.

"I know, but I wanted to," I said with a shrug.

"I don't get you," he said with a sigh, putting down his menu.

I peered at him over mine. "What do you mean?"

"I mean, for starters you're... well... you," he said as he gestured to me.

Raising an eyebrow, I couldn't help but smirk.

"Are you always this articulate, Taylor, or has the coffee not settled in yet?"

He furrowed his brows, twisting his lips as he nipped, "Fuck you, Drew."

"Only if you buy me dinner first," I teased, flashing him a wink.

He sighed in exasperation. "You are insufferable, you know that," he said as he picked up his menu again, just as the waitress came by to take our orders.

When she'd gone and we'd ordered half the menu, he spoke again.

"What I mean is... you waltz around here like you're nobody, like you're just some guy and not the front man of a band that's gone platinum like, twelve times."

Ah, so does know more than he lets on.

"I told you, *Axe 2 Grind* is my job. It's not who I am." The words were true, but somehow they felt heavier than all the other times I'd said them. "I mean, you aren't your job, right? There's the you that you reserve for work, and the you that you reserve for other people, your friends."

For the person you love.

Taylor sipped his coffee, his shoulders loosening as he closed his eyes and let out a groan of satisfaction that went straight to my cock.

Not now...

I stirred my own cup of coffee, if only because I needed to focus on something else other than the sound of his satisfied moaning and my cock that was lamenting its own memory of the sound.

"Yes, but my job isn't nearly as... glamorous as yours. I'm not jet setting across the world to play sold out shows and dating *America's Sexiest Man Alive.*"

His words cut through my heart like a knife, and I bristled at the title, as well as his insinuation.

"*Was* dating America's Sexiest Man Alive. Until he fucking cheated on me with his co-worker."

I watched Taylor's eyes widen as my words settled on him.

"You're not—"

"No. I'm not. And I haven't been with anyone since we broke up." I felt like I needed to say that. I'm not sure if it was for my own belief or if it was for Taylor, for him to understand that what happened between us wasn't just some drunk rockstar party bullshit.

I liked him. I could admit that, but I got the feeling that Taylor admitting he actually *liked me* wasn't quite an easy thing for him to confess. But the way he looked at me when I said 'no, we are not together', was full of relief and understanding, and I knew despite his outward behaviors, his bite, he did in fact *like me.*

DREW

"And we are never, ever, getting back together," I said with a smirk, if only to alleviate the tension that had befallen us.

Thankfully, Taylor got my reference, letting out a small laugh.

"Even if he calls you up like, 'I still love you'?" he said with a smirk of his own.

I couldn't help but smile. "I mean, this is exhausting."

Taylor shook his head, rolling his eyes. "Like I said, insufferable."

"Well, well, good morning you two." Giselle's voice broke the energy that formed between us, pulling us both to where she and Julie stood, looking just as put together as they had last night before things got...

Messy.

They looked ten times better than I suspected they felt, if Taylor's hangover was just as bad.

"Good... morning..." Taylor spoke, his voice far away.

"I hope Helena took good care of you," I said, flashing them with a bright smile and I watched Julie's smile widen.

"Very," she said, shooting Taylor an accusatory glance.

While I hadn't given Taylor an NDA, or the girls, I didn't worry that he would divulge what had happened between us, from the sheer fact he seemed to want to do the very opposite under Julie's gaze.

"Rough night, Tay?" she said with a smirk.

Taylor took a sip from his coffee cup before answering.

"You could say that," he drawled, shifting his stance in his seat like a scolded child.

"Join us," I said, noting the other two chairs set at our table.

"Oh, I couldn't intrude..." Julie said sweetly. "Not after everything else you've already done."

"Absolutely," Giselle said over her

friend, pulling up a chair with a smile on her face. "But this one's on me," she said as she got comfortable.

Taylor looked as if he wanted to head for the hills as Julie pulled up a chair next him.

The three of them together in the space, looked absolutely perfect. Like they were some serialized modern version of *Three's Company,* complete with the successful woman who has it all, the gay bestie, and the *fun* one.

Sitting in Paradise, watching you shine like a star.

The lyrics came to me almost instantly as I watched Taylor sip his coffee, Julie wrapping her arm around him in a hug while Giselle cracked a smile.

I hummed the words as I slid my phone out to record them. Just before I went to put it away, on a whim, I decided to encapsulate the moment, if only to provide me with more inspiration later.

"Say I'm hungover," I teased and the girls laughed. Taylor rolled his eyes, but the girls squeezed in and he smirked.

Click!

I couldn't help but smile too, because for the first time in a long time I felt like I was finally *happy*.

And when Taylor caught me staring over a fresh plate of eggs, bacon, and avocado toast, the sparkle in his eyes led me to believe even if he denied it, he was happy too.

CHAPTER NINETEEN

Drew

I WATCHED, FEELING sadness as the trio headed off through the lobby to pick up the Uber Helena had called for them.

Truth was, I had more fun singing karaoke and drinking on my bus with Giselle, Julie, and Taylor than any party in LA.

I wished in that moment, as I watched Taylor turn to wave goodbye, that I could stay.

That things could be different for me.

"Should I be worried about that one?" Helena said calmly as I waved back.

"No," I said smoothly. "I don't think we have to worry about him, or the girls."

"Good. Because I have a last minute cancellation, and the Brisby Ballfield has an opening tomorrow night."

I raised an eyebrow as I looked at her. "I thought we tried to book Brisby and they were filled."

Howler smiled wide. "We did, but they had some sort of corporate event. I guess the event was canceled because of some corporate bs, so they have an opening tomorrow night and called me just this morning and wanted to know if you'd be able to fill in."

"That's not even enough time to sell tickets."

Howler shrugged as she pulled out her phone, taking a photograph of me before sweetly replying, "Come hang out with

Drew Axel at the Brisby Ballfield, tomorrow night for a *free concert* at eight pm!"

"You said yes already didn't you?" I asked, knowing the answer. No one knew my schedule better than she did, and she booked all my appearances, even the ones on the sordid talk shows.

"Maybe..."

I sighed as I nodded. "Guess I don't have much of a choice then," I vented.

"Oh, stop acting like I busted your Legos, Axel. You've been going on and on about how much you *loved* this place and missed it, and how you wanted to just kick back for a bit, so I thought you'd appreciate us staying in town a little longer to give you a little bit of time off."

"Working three shows almost back to back is the exact opposite of time off, Howler."

"Psssh. You ain't forty yet, baby. Plus, you know you love it." Her eyes lit up as she got an idea. "Oh, maybe you can do a total cover show tomorrow night. Sing some of those Taylor Swift songs you think I don't hear you humming all the time," she said as she pushed me in the shoulder.

"Yeah, because the masses will *love* that."

"I mean, she is trending *all over* Instagram and TikTok right now, it couldn't hurt to join the Taylor train. Might get us some good likes and publicity."

Just what I wanted. More publicity.

"Tomorrow, huh? So what's on the agenda for today then?" I asked.

She shrugged, flipping her hair over her shoulder.

"I don't have anything on my calendar since it was originally supposed to be a travel day, but even with the Ballfield event tomorrow, we don't have another main show until Tuesday next week, so...

maybe you could actually relax today? Curl up in your bed with some Doritos and watch movies. I know how much you love watching movies in fancy hotels," she said, flashing me a grin.

She wasn't wrong, but something about the way she said the words made me feel sad.

Alone.

I used to love venturing out into the cities I played in, but ever since I'd been with Rozen, I stopped venturing out, and spent most of my time at the gym or at health retreats with him. And when I did get time to myself, all I wanted to do was everything I *couldn't* do with him.

Eat junk food.

Watch dumb rom-coms.

Chill the fuck out and just sit on the porch and play my guitar.

Alone.

Hope blossomed in my chest that maybe... just maybe, I could see if Taylor wanted to hang out.

But I didn't even have his number, not that I couldn't find it but...

A text notification popped up from Giselle.

Hey, I just wanted to let you know we all got home and are good, and I sincerely appreciate you putting us all up last night. I can't believe how messed up we got. I haven't drank that much since college.

I texted her back, as a plan formed in my brain.

Glad to hear you guys are good, and it's fine. I'm glad you had fun, and we had something to celebrate. Taylor okay?

"Sure," I said, as I smiled at Howler, who was giving me a suspicious look.

"Mhmmm. Just be on your best behavior, yeah?" she said, her voice carrying a hint of excitement.

Taylor is fine, why?

A devilish grin spread on my face.

Because I still have his flannel and I

wanted to return it to him.

It seemed an eternity until she answered.

He left his shirt on your bus? Damn, that's classic!

I rolled my eyes. I doubted that he'd left it *on purpose.* After all, it was quite a bit chaotic this morning, but a part of me, the hopeless romantic, dared to dream it was purposeful.

Because it would mean he wanted to see me again, too.

I'm going to be around at least until tomorrow, got a last-minute gig, so I thought I'd pop by his shop later and drop it off.

Giselle texted me back his shop address and number with several heart eyes emojis.

It's not like that, I swear. Even though I desperately hoped it was, or that it could be.

She only sent me a string of eggplant

emojis and more heart eyes, followed by a kissy face, and I couldn't help but laugh.

You like him.

It wasn't a question as much as a statement.

I knew I should deny my feelings for the snarky, hot florist.

I knew I should put what happened between us out of my mind.

But something about the way Giselle, even after twenty-some years, could read me like a book made me feel seen and heard, and I didn't want to fabricate the truth anymore.

It's... complicated.

Giselle's eyeroll emoji stared blankly at me as she typed away.

Did you... she sent me an eggplant emoji.

I thought about lying.

But this wasn't the first time Giselle and I played this game, and I knew better than to lie to one of the only people on the planet who could see through all my bullshit.

I don't kiss and tell, G. You know that.

A steady string of hearts fluttered across my screen with very large caps OMGs.

Like I said, it's complicated.

Whatever you say... AJ Andrews. Followed with a winking emoji.

I smiled at the use of my name, laughing, if only because it was apparent she had caught me creeping on her profile with my secret profile.

But if anything, her use of my childhood moniker only solidified my confidence that my secrets truly were safe with her, so I slid my phone back in my pocket, excused myself from Helena's sights, and headed to my tour bus in search of Taylor's flannel.

CHAPTER TWENTY

Taylor

"I NEED ALL the details, Tay. Come on, pleeeeease," Julie whined as we walked up my sidewalk.

I'd told the Uber to leave, and offered to take Julie home myself, after I'd showered of course. I passed her house on the way to work every day anyway.

"Nothing happened," I lied.

But like the super sleuth she was, Julie only called my bluff.

"Really? Then where's your flannel? Still hanging on Drew's bedpost, I take it?" she teased.

My cheeks instantly flushed at her words, which was a dead giveaway.

Damn it!

All at once, I closed my eyes as I realized in my hurry to leave his tour bus, I had almost left my phone, and I'd been in such a mood, feeling like shit I hadn't even *looked* for my flannel. I'd just thrown the rest of my clothes on and tried to get as far away as I could.

Because I knew no matter how I felt, how sexy and intriguing I thought Drew was, that things could never work between us.

For starters, I'd already moved once because of a man, and I wasn't intent on moving again. I'd worked hard to set up my life in Jasper Springs, to build my shop from the ground up. It might not have been much, but it was *mine*, and I was damn proud of it.

Not to mention, Drew had his own life. Sold out shows and photoshoots, and rubbing elbows with Hollywood.

In what world would someone like him want a lazy, small town life where nothing exciting happened?

Well, nothing exciting until a hot rockstar comes to town.

"Doubt it. We didn't make it to the bed," I grumbled under my breath. "More like just the couch." My cheeks flushed as I realized I'd slipped up.

Oops, guess the cat is out of the bag now.

Julie squealed as she pulled me close on my porch, her body practically vibrating.

"Oh my God, Taylor! I knew you had it in you!" she said, letting out a laugh.

I sighed in defeat, bringing my arms up to hug her. The relief that came over me was somewhat cathartic.

"Thanks but, I don't exactly feel all that great," I said.

"Why not? Was it... not a good experience? Did he get like... whiskey dick? Or did you? I mean, we were all pretty drunk and—"

"No, that's not the problem," I said, feeling flushed again.

Julie steamrolled through my discomfort like a dog with a bone, intent on getting the full story. Her blue eyes glittered with the promise of sordid details.

"Then what is?"

The fact I couldn't articulate exactly *what* was bothering me about what had happened, or how I felt about it, was gnawing at me.

I unlocked my door, focusing on my key as Julie pressed on.

"Because if this is some 'I don't deserve him because he's a big star and I'm not' bullshit, I'm going to smack you."

DREW

I opened the door, waving her in with a scowl.

"It's complicated, okay?" I said as I closed the door, Julie finding her spot on my couch as I headed for the fridge to grab a bottle of water.

"It's not. You just need to realize not every man you're attracted to is *Zack*," she said softly.

Just hearing his name out loud made it feel like I couldn't breathe. I stopped, looking at Julie's watery blue eyes as she held my gaze.

I'd been heartbroken to start out my life in Jasper Springs, alone, and the camaraderie I felt with Giselle and Julie was too addicting to refuse. I'd told them about my ex, not in great detail, but they knew the gist. That we'd broken up and I moved to Jasper Springs.

That he wanted to chase his dreams, and I wasn't one of them.

"I know that," I said, swallowing

harshly, but even I didn't believe my own words.

"Did it ever occur to you that maybe he actually does you know... like *you*?"

I rolled my eyes. "You've known the man for less than twenty-four hours and you know everything about him, right?" My words sounded bitter even to me, but I couldn't help the anxiety swelling in my stomach.

Julie shrugged it off though. "I know that he was looking at you like a fresh serving of apple pie," she said, flashing me a smirk. "And that was just during the show. When you were singing... Hell, I wish *any* man would look at me like that."

My shoulders fell, and hope threatened to blossom in my heart.

His words filled my brain from our breakfast, how he'd told me that he hadn't actually been with anyone since his break up, and quoted my favorite singer. How, despite my bristly attitude toward him, he'd been nothing but kind and sweet.

Which I didn't deserve in the least.

I've been such a fucking asshole.

"Yeah, well, I haven't exactly been the sweetest peach, so don't get your hopes up," I said as I tossed a bottle of water to her.

"Taylor..."

"I'm getting a shower, then we'll head out," I said, avoiding the conversation, the feels, like the plague.

Once I'd popped some Advil and gotten in the shower, I felt like I could finally relax. Under the steady stream of hot water, I felt like I could breathe, could process everything that had happened in the last forty-eight hours.

Showing up to M's Place and seeing Drew for the first time.

Drew showing up to the shop with Giselle, and him singing Taylor Swift.

The taste of his lips against mine, the

feel of his cock against my own.

The way he looked hurt at my insinuations.

The look of sadness on his face as he waved goodbye to me.

I braced my hands against the tiles, letting out a shaky breath as his memory filled my consciousness.

His *reputation* tattoo, among all the others, stood out to me as familiar lyrics filled my brain.

About having big reputations, big enemies, and that being a big, big conversation.

I doubted Taylor Swift was singing about her own self-destructive resolve.

Maybe Julie was right. Maybe I was being too guarded, too closed off. But I didn't know *how* to open up after I'd spent so many years protecting my heart. I didn't know how to let anyone in, especially a tall, dark, and hot rockstar who I just couldn't seem to stay away from.

Which is why I planned on focusing on the things I *could* control today, and that was work. Perhaps sorting and designing the arrangements for the Anderson funeral I hadn't gotten to last night—because I'd agreed to close up shop early and go out with my friends for a night—would help me feel better about the fact I was probably never going to see Drew Axel again, and I'd been a complete asshole.

Not to mention there was no way I was getting my flannel back now.

CHAPTER TWENTY-ONE

Taylor

I'D OVERESTIMATED THE amount of orders, not to mention while I was gone, between the hours of last night and this morning, someone had put through *four* online orders for the Anderson event, and they weren't *easy* arrangements.

The shop was a mess, I was out of iced coffee, and I was sorely cursing myself for not being a responsible adult and just not getting wasted last night.

With a hot musician.

Who you're probably never going to see again except in your fucking dreams.

So, imagine my surprise when the door swung open to reveal a dark figure, clad in ripped black jeans and a Ouija print muscle tank, carrying two iced coffees with my flannel draped over his right biceps; the one with the hot, thick vein...

You're hallucinating.

You have to be.

It's probably the stress of everything, of this fucking day...

"Hi," he said awkwardly as he looked around the room.

"Hi..." I said, feeling rather on the spot. There were a hundred things I wanted to say, but instead I said, "Do you need something, or..."

"I... oh, uh... right," he said as he scowled at the messy studio. "Is... is this a bad time," he asked.

I sighed, waltzing up to him, both

irritated and relieved to have a caffeine fix.

And maybe because he truly was a sight for sore eyes.

"What do you think?" I said as I crossed my arms, glancing down at the coffee. "You trying to buy my silence?"

"Oh, uh... no. No, shit. I didn't mean—"

All at once, Julie's words came back to me and I had to wonder if she was right. My heart dared to hope maybe there was a sliver of truth to her words.

Maybe this lumbering tower of sex appeal actually *was* just a nice guy under all the tats and abs.

And here I was, again, being a complete dick.

"Don't you have like, employees to help you?" he asked cautiously.

I scoffed at his remark. "Not for this sort of thing. I'm a one-man show," I huffed as he handed me the coffee, our fingers touching as he did so.

"I mean, Julie has a key, and sometimes she helps me out when I get really backed up, but she's working today and the kid who usually runs my deliveries isn't picking up his phone, and—"

"I can help," he said, heading straight for the counter, setting down my flannel and his drink in the process.

I couldn't help the surprise in my voice as I gasped, following him like a moth to a black flame.

"You? Help? What do you know about floral arranging?" I scoffed. I took another pull of my iced coffee, relishing in the sweet taste on my tongue that made me feel a bit more relaxed almost immediately.

Drew cast me a smirk as he started lining up the long-stemmed flowers I hadn't cut yet for a wreath arrangement.

"I had a girlfriend in high school. Her mom used to make all the arrangements for the local dances and stuff. I used to help her out sometimes, even after we broke up."

My mouth opened in surprise, and I realized I must have been staring when he looked at me puzzled.

"What?"

"Girlfriend?" I asked, feeling strangely on the spot. As if the reality dawned on him, he shook his head.

"I mean, I tried pussy. Like, a lot, and its not bad, sometimes, but I *prefer* dick," he said, flashing me a mischievous grin.

"So, all the women you've been... er... linked with, you've..."

Drew pushed some things around on the counter, before I asked, "Are you looking for something?"

"Clippers. I need to trim these stems," he said, looking at me as if I should have known.

The sight only made me want to put him in his place.

And his comment about preferring dick, well...

I handed him the scissors, and he set to work.

I was impressed that he actually trimmed them perfectly.

"Not all of them. Just a few. Like I said, I prefer—"

"The tabloids tend to depict you as a bit of a manwhore," I said.

Drew shrugged. "I prefer the term *experienced*."

"There are levels of experience you know," I grumbled. "So that doesn't actually convey what you think it does," I said.

Drew laughed. "I mean, you didn't seem to complain too much about my *experience* last night when I made you come. Twice, if I remember correctly."

You are insufferable," I said as I started working on the arrangement he was laying the flowers out for.

DREW

"So I've been told," he said, following with a sly grin that actually made me feel at ease.

I took my spot behind the counter as he trimmed the flowers, making a pile that I could easily pull from as I worked to arrange the wreath to the picture.

Silence befell us but it wasn't awkward. In fact, it was kind of peaceful once we'd found a rhythm, a system, working like a well-oiled machine.

Like he'd always been there with me.

My heart lurched as I stole a glance at him. Amidst all the pastels and light filtering in, he looked almost ominous, every bit like a rock and roll demon or a bad boy straight from a romance novel.

But there was a softness to him too; in his thick eyelashes and the way they contrasted his pale skin, the way the corners of his eyes bore the sight of slight creases. The rough definition of his long, calloused fingers covered in tattoos.

For a man close to forty—thirty-eight, if the Internet was indeed correct—he had an effervescent youthfulness to him that was difficult not to notice.

And maybe that was why I decided to break the silence, why I decided to turn over and bare the one thing I'd protected for so long to him.

"Drew, about last night..."

"It's fine, I get it. You don't have to say anything," he said quietly as he clipped another carnation stem. "I'm used to being a regret, so you don't have to—"

"No, I was... I was a dick to you. Not just last night, but in general. I haven't been the most welcoming individual. Honestly, I don't know why you give me the time of day at all considering I've practically roasted you at every turn."

Drew cast me a wicked smile that I suppose would have melted any panties in my vicinity if there were some.

"*Experience* has taught me I have a bit

of a degradation kink," he murmured haughtily, the sound of his voice immediately causing my cock to twitch and my cheeks to burn scarlet. "And maybe I'm developing a kink for grumpy, hot florists."

Somebody fucking pinch me!

"Tell you what," he said as he slid over the last bundle of cut flowers. "Why don't we start over? A fresh start."

I looked at him across the table as I set my hand over the bundle, slowly pulling it toward me.

"I guess that wouldn't be a terrible idea," I said cautiously.

"How does dinner sound?" he asked, shifting his weight.

I moved around the corner with the completed wreath, toward the side door where the delivery van waited for me to load the last few arrangements.

"That sounds nice but, I, uh, have to get these off to the funeral home, but I'm free after seven?" I said, swallowing my nerves.

"What's good around here? I, uh, haven't really gotten to explore much since I've been here," he said sheepishly as he followed me toward the van with another arrangement.

Once we'd loaded them in the van, I turned to face him, the sunlight falling over him, and making him look every bit like the man of my dreams, gold halo and all.

"Well, not much unless you like pizza, BBQ, Chinese, or cafe food."

"Pizza does sound really good, actually. I can't remember the last time I had a good, cheesy, hot slice," he said thoughtfully.

"Okay, so, seven at Jasper Springs Pizza?" I asked nervously, my palms already starting to sweat.

Drew cracked a smile as he nodded. "It's a date."

CHAPTER TWENTY-TWO

Taylor

I PACED BACK and forth in my townhouse, feeling my nerves getting the best of me. I couldn't stop thinking about Drew or what he called our *date.*

It wasn't a date though, right?

It was just two guys starting over, starting fresh, hanging out over pizza.

Right?

So, I did the only thing I could think of that might actually make my stomach calm down, and I called Julie.

Who picked up on the first ring.

"Hey, Tay, what's—"

"I'm meeting Drew Axel for pizza in a half hour and I think I'm going to pass the fuck out," was all I managed to get out of my mouth.

"You what? Oh my God, Taylor. What... How..."

"He, uh, came by the shop earlier to, you know, uh, drop off my flannel and some coffee, and well, things just kinda—"

"I knew it! He likes you!"

"I mean, it was left on his bus," I mused as I caught a glimpse of myself in the mirror. Despite the heat and panic I felt, I didn't look like I was having a mental breakdown, so that was a plus.

I'd gone with a more casual look, since I wasn't all that sure my usual khakis and fancy button down wedding-esque attire would match the small town aesthetic of Jasper Springs Pizza.

Instead, I'd opted for a simple blue tee shirt, a pair of dark wash jeans, and my black and white Converse that I never really wore anymore. Combined with my casual, just brushed hair, I looked like someone else. Someone I hadn't seen in years.

I looked like the Taylor Meade I was when I'd arrived here, in Jasper Springs.

Young, hopeful.

"Yeah, and that smitten kitten brought it back with coffee, and asked you out? So, I'd say whatever you're doing is working and I might need to bottle some of it up for my damn self," she teased.

"I just... like, what if it's a bad idea?" I said as I collapsed on my oversized livingroom chair.

"I beg your pardon?" she blurted.

"What if... I mean, it's not like he *lives* here. He's just... he's a rockstar. Traveling is like, his job, and he's just going to leave in a day or two, and—"

And I don't want to get my heart broken a second time.

Julie sighed. "Taylor," she said calmly.

I closed my eyes as I tried to fight through the panic and anxiety flooding me. "Yeah, Jules?"

"It's okay to have fun. It's okay to just enjoy the moment. With a guy you like, who obviously likes you."

"But—"

"Nothing is certain, Tay. All we have is *the moment.* So, do as your patron saint would, and be *fearless.* Live in the moment. Just for tonight, okay?"

I sighed as Julie's words hit me, knowing just the song she was referencing.

Fearless.

I glanced at the clock on my end table, noting I had less than twenty minutes.

"Are you still there, Tay?" she asked quietly, and I nodded, even though she couldn't see me.

DREW

"Yeah, I, uh, gotta go, Jules. Thanks," I said, and hung up.

I sucked in a deep breath, and left the comfort of my humble abode, venturing into the unknown with a thudding heart, and a wish that maybe Julie was right.

Maybe tonight would be the best night ever, but I'd never know if I didn't make it there, right?

CHAPTER TWENTY-THREE

Taylor

I FOUND DREW in the corner of Jasper Springs Pizza, alone in a corner booth, looking quite different than usual. For starters, he was wearing *clothes*.

His ripped jeans had been replaced with simple dark wash jeans like mine, and he'd traded in his muscle tank for a simple, understated, black fitted tee. The shirt alone drew attention to the definition of his muscles, making his myriad of tattoos much brighter.

His dark hair was swept back casually, just a few kamikaze strands hanging in front of his bright green eyes. When he looked up at me, the hint of a smile pulling at the corner of his lips, whatever ice had surrounded my heart instantly melted.

He wasn't even wearing any eyeliner, and I could see his thick, full lashes on display, making him all the more endearing and... seductive.

He looked...

Beautiful.

"Hey," I said, my voice cracking as I caught his gaze.

"Hey," he said as I slid into my seat.

"Everything go okay with your delivery?" he asked as he reached over to grab his glass, which looked like Coke.

"Yeah, for the most part," I said as the waitress came over to take our order. "What about you? What have you been up to for the past five hours?" I asked, trying my hardest to sound coherent, since I hadn't really flirted or gone on a date in seven years.

God, take me now.

"Set up the set list, did some TikToks. Howler added a show at the Brisby Ballfield tomorrow. Kind of a last minute thing."

"Oh," I said as the waitress dropped off my drink of Root Beer.

"Is that something that happens often?" I asked, not wanting to ask the real question on my mind.

Julie said to just live in the moment, don't worry about the future.

Drew shrugged. "Sometimes, yeah. Less likely when I'm with the band, but this solo tour is kind of different. It's more about small towns. Back to my roots, sort of thing, so it's kinda fitting I'll be playing at the ball field I used to hang out at. Twenty years ago, anyway."

"I'm not really all that familiar with everything around here," I admitted as I stirred my straw in my drink.

"Transplant?" he asked as he scooted closer to me in the booth. I pretended not to notice, even though my cock very much noticed his proximity.

Down boy!

That's not what we're here for!

I moved an inch closer, if only because I couldn't help myself. Drew... er, Axel, just had this magnetic field to him that seemed to suck me in no matter what, and I hated to admit, I kind of liked it.

It made me feel safe.

Like as long as I was with him, I could just let my guard down.

"Yeah, I, uh, moved here about seven years ago, after..." I held my breath as the words caught in my throat.

Aside from Julie and Giselle, I didn't really have friends, and even though I had told them the basics, I'd never really talked about what happened in detail. But sitting in Jasper Springs Pizza with a gorgeous man sitting beside me, I felt compelled to tell him.

I knew trusting a rockstar was dangerous. Hell, giving up any part of myself to anyone was dangerous, but I also had the startling feeling Axel, of all people, would understand for some reason.

"After my ex left me to go to Hollywood. To be a *star*." I glanced up at Drew, noting the wistfulness in his eyes as my words settled on him.

"A star, huh?" He huffed, pursing his lips.

"Yeah, he, uh, had this dream that he was going to be like, the next Adam Levine or something, and I guess I was just holding him back." I sighed.

"Dreams don't mean anything if you don't have someone to share them with," he said as he moved closer, setting his palm on my thigh.

My heart was racing, thudding so loud against my chest, like a drum, I wondered if he could hear it. Nervously, I thought about Taylor's words. About being led headfirst into the unknown, and I bit my lip as those words fueled me to take a chance.

To set my hand on top of his.

I intertwined my fingers with his, feeling his warm palm against my fingertips, and I let out a heavy breath.

"Sometimes, dreams are all we have," I breathed. "And I don't regret it, staying here in Jasper Springs to build *my dream.* It led me to Giselle and Julie, and..."

To you.

To this moment in time.

Drew squeezed my hand, and I hoped he could feel what I didn't have the courage to say.

"Oh my God! Drew Axel, is that you?" A high-pitched squeal shattered the overwhelming tension between us and I quickly slipped my hand away, my gaze flashing to a woman bouncing up and down with her camera in her hand.

Drew slid his hand back to his lap, his gaze shifting, his smile brighter.

I watched as he turned off himself, shifting into the man the world knew as Drew Axel right before my eyes.

And a part of me hated it.

Because I wanted *him* all to myself.

"You bet your ass, sweetheart," he said, and he stuck his tongue out at her.

I watched as she blushed, squealing some more.

"Oh my God, can I get a picture? Please? I'm a huge fan!" she gushed, and he smiled at me, though his eyes weren't as bright as his smile. He turned to her, nodding in approval as he scooted out of the booth.

"Of course!" he said as she positioned her camera for a selfie, making a kissy duckface and throwing up a peace sign like a basic bitch.

I rolled my eyes.

"Under one condition," he said as he smiled and she clicked.

"Oh my God, of course! Anything!" she said as she took another, before sliding her phone in her pocket.

I watched as Drew slid his phone out, swiped it open and handed it to her.

"Can you take a picture of me and my friend here?"

Friend.

The word made me feel a complex mixture of emotions, everything from anger to satisfaction. Because he saw me as a friend. Someone worthy of helping out, someone he could have coffee and pizza with.

But at that moment, I knew I loved him because I didn't want to be his friend.

I wanted to be more than *friends*.

I wanted to be unequivocally *his*.

"Of course!" she said with another high-pitched squeal as Drew held his hand out to me. His bright eyes shone with warmth and I looked from him to his hand, feeling like this was some sort of test.

Some sort of threshold into the unknown.

But damn it if I wasn't a glutton for wanting things I shouldn't, for flying too close to fire.

I set my hand in his, letting him pull me up.

"Stand right here..." he said as he set both his hands on my arms, shifting me into place in front of the table.

"Oh... okay..." I said, swallowing nervously.

"Perfect," he said as he trailed his fingers down my arm before taking his spot next to me. He threw his arm around my shoulders, pulling me close.

So close I could smell his musky

cologne, his spicy hair product, and get a nice, close up of the word that taunted me on his neck.

Reputation.

Boy, you and me would be a big conversation.

I hesitantly settled my hand around his waist, hovering my hand just a hair above his hip.

Drew tightened his grip as he leaned his head against mine, flashing a smile for the camera. But I missed it.

Because I couldn't take my eyes off of him.

"Can we get one more?" he asked, flashing the fan a bright smile. The happy blonde nodded in approval as he whispered in my ear, "You are the prettiest thing in this room, you know that, right?"

I couldn't help but blush at his words, his hot breath on my neck stirring my unruly cock once more, making my stomach tie in knots.

I knew it could just be words. That Axel was *experienced* and knew his way around flattery probably as much as he did a dick, but I also felt the strangest hint of sincerity in his voice at his words, and couldn't help the shit-eating grin that crossed my face.

"I know," I said as I adjusted my stance, aiming my gaze at the fan who clicked the button.

She handed his phone back with another squeal, scampering off to leave us be.

The momentary boost of confidence I had settled as our waitress brought our dinner, but I still felt the pang of uncertainty, the sting of anxiety poking me.

Because this... this is who Drew Axel was. This was his life.

And that would never change, even if I wanted it to.

Even if I believed for a moment, he wasn't some rockstar, that he was just a deliciously hot, tattooed Swiftie who liked to sing and knew how to arrange flowers, and looked hot in a muscle tank or with a guitar between his legs.

"Well, uh, thanks for everything," I said as I finished my last slice of pizza, knowing that this almost perfect moment in time would soon come to an end, and it was better to cut things off before I fell over the hill and into the point of no return.

"What? You think this date is over already? Are you Cinderella? Do you turn into a pumpkin or something if you're out past your bedtime?" he teased, his lips pulling up into a scandalous smile.

"No, I just, uh, I wasn't aware this was an actual *date*," I said, hurriedly adding, "I mean, I haven't like, been on a date in awhile and..."

Oh my God Taylor, just stop talking.

DREW

Don't make it awkward...

Drew smiled as he signed the receipt, which I'd vehemently tried to pick up, but he refused to let me.

"Nonsense," he'd said. "Let me take care of you. I mean, I kind of had a whole thing planned..." he said as he slipped his hands in his pockets.

"You... did?" I asked, dumbfounded.

He nodded in response. "Yeah, and you know, I'd really hate to go to *SLAM!* by myself," he whined, pouting at me with exaggeration like a small child.

I couldn't help but laugh as I shoved him in the arm. "Does that look really work for you, Axel?" I retorted.

He grinned wickedly. "Yes, as a matter of fact it does."

"You are insufferable," I said, shaking my head as he walked ahead of me.

"Come on, gorgeous. This night's just getting started."

CHAPTER TWENTY-FOUR

Drew

I COULDN'T REMEMBER the last time I felt like myself, not the way I felt when I was with Taylor.

Since that very first night, where I'd picked him out of a crowd to perform to, he'd treated me like I wasn't anything special, which for someone of my celebrity was saying something.

I knew most A-list celebs like Rozen would have scoffed at such behavior—not to mention stirred up enough heat in the media to keep the press talking—but for me, it was actually kind of a relief.

I'd spent the last twenty years of my life being someone else, and perhaps at times, I truly believed it was who I was.

But being home, in Jasper Springs, walking around with Giselle, singing karaoke on my bus, and hanging out with Taylor was more than a breath of fresh air for me.

It was *cathartic.*

And I wanted more of it. I never wanted my time with the grouchy, *endearing* florist to end.

I almost worried that I'd fucked up when I took that fan's autograph in the pizza shop. Granted, most of my time in Jasper Springs had been pretty low-key, but it was bound to happen sooner or later. But right before it did, Taylor had done the unthinkable. He opened up.

To *me.*

The fact was not lost on me, as I got the impression both from his profile, and just from the time I'd actually spent with him—when his cock wasn't being shoved down my throat—that he wasn't the type to wear his heart on his sleeve. Not like me.

No, Taylor bravely showed his true colors to me, and I was hooked.

As if I hadn't been before.

"What is this place?" he asked as we exited the Uber.

"They're running a show tonight on Georgia O'Keefe's 'secret' paintings," I said with a shrug. "Thought it might be up your alley." I flashed him a smirk. "You do know who she is, right?" I teased, and Taylor took my bait. I swear I loved to push his buttons, get that grumpy attitude going.

Like I said, it's a bit of a kink.

"Of course I know who she is! Only an uncultured swine would question such a thing!" he said as he shoved me in the arm.

He's so perfect.

"Then by all means, lead the way," I said as I waved toward the entrance.

Taylor took off, and I followed, adjusting my shades as we entered the swanky *Rhodes Gallery*. I'd never been one for art shows, but the fact the place was showcasing paintings of a famous floral painter, I knew I couldn't pass up the chance to bring Taylor.

The gallery itself was next to *SLAM!*, a poetry cafe, and it was open mic night, so I thought some dinner, some art, and maybe a romantic poetry reading would be just the sort of thing to get Taylor to open up, and have some fun.

Okay, and maybe I wanted to get back to my roots too.

After all, I started out writing poetry before I moved to writing my own songs.

The light in the gallery was bright, and

it lit up Taylor like some sort of angel. Dressed in his dark jeans and a dark blue shirt, with the light kissing his sandy hair, his blue eyes stood out like O' Keefe's painting of a morning glory, aptly titled *Morning Glory.*

I slowly followed behind Taylor, who was looking at everything with wide eyes and wonder, and I couldn't help but feel like I was seeing something rare.

For a moment, I felt like an observer rather than an icon, and I liked how that felt. To just blend in between the walls of paintings.

When he finally stopped, I did too, taking a quiet stance beside him. He stared at the painting in front of us, a close up image that I couldn't really make out. The long brush strokes and shapes gave it a feminine shape, the stamen in the center poised with a little, yellow bead that reminded me of...

"It looks like a vag," I whispered,

leaning against him.

Taylor shot me a dirty look. "Well, you would know, I suppose," he quipped, before adding, "But, that's kind of the point. O'Keefe was known to push the sexual connotations with a lot of her paintings."

"I knew that," I said nonchalantly. "I was just, you know, testing you."

"Mhmm. I'm starting to think degradation isn't your only kink, Axel. I think you just like to be a pain in my ass."

"Maybe I want you to be a pain in *my* ass, *Tay*," I said as I walked away, leaving him to stand there gaping at me.

"You are..."

"Insufferable. Yeah, I know, so you say. But I'm not the one who's following me through a room full of pussy paintings," I teased as I scampered off in the other direction.

Taylor shook his head as he jogged to

catch up with me. I tried my best to not run, after all, I didn't want to get thrown out of the gallery, but there was something freeing and fun about dodging Taylor through the other visitors, around walls and in tiny crevices.

When we finally found each other once more, in a secluded corner that boasted a painting that looked like a sort of sunset and not a flower, he was grinning ear to ear.

"I was going to say, you are something else, Axel," he said as he backed me against the wall. He pressed his body against me, not harshly, but with just enough pressure to show me he meant business.

Well, kinky business anyway, since I knew there was no way in hell Taylor wanted to hurt me.

I set my hand on his hip, nudging him closer, pressing my twitching cock against him. When I felt his reciprocated hardness, I smiled wickedly.

"I know," I said, my gaze dipping to his lips.

Taylor shook his head as he set his hand against the wall by my head, letting out a deep breath. For a moment, I could see the excitement, the same wonder and awe in his eyes when he looked at *me*, like he had when he looked at Georgia's paintings.

I leaned in just a hair, parting my lips, and that flash disappeared as someone rounded the corner, causing both of us to detach, to stifle our probably inappropriate hard-ons.

"I, uh... think we should—"

"Mhmm, couldn't agree more," I said as I grabbed his hand without thinking, leading him through the rest of the exhibit.

CHAPTER TWENTY-FIVE

Drew

"WELL, THAT WAS..."

"Enlightening?" I asked as I led us next door to *SLAM!*, stopping just in front of the cafe window. Inside, the world was shades of amber and ochre, and there was a rather decent sized crowd filling the floor and tables.

"I was going to say unexpected, but enlightening works too, I guess," he said as I nodded at the cafe.

"Fancy a... iced coffee, is it?" I said, cocking my head to the side.

"Sure, why not," he said, flashing me with a grin.

"I like to see you smile," I said like an idiot.

Real smooth, Drew.

"I am actually having a great time, so..." Taylor said with a blush creeping over his cheeks.

Overhead, I could hear the familiar lyrics of my favorite Taylor Swift ballad, *Wildest Dreams*.

I looked at Taylor in the light of the cafe's entrance, as gallery goers spilled out of the Rhodes Gallery behind us, and I couldn't deny the truth in her words.

It was getting good.

And I didn't want it to end.

I moved to open the door for him, waving him in.

"It's only the truth, baby, promise," I said, following with a flirtatious wink.

Taylor found us a table near the front, and it wasn't long until someone came to take our orders.

"It's, uh, open mic night tonight, so if I'm correct, in about five minutes, they'll open up the stage."

Taylor leaned back in his chair, crossing his jean-clad legs as he raised an eyebrow.

"Which means you're going up there, right?"

"Am I that transparent?" I asked, running a hand through my hair.

"Can take the man out of the music, but not the music out of the man, right?"

I cocked a smile at his relaxed humor. I liked seeing him undone, unraveling for me.

And I certainly felt inspired by such things.

By him.

"You could go up there too, you know. I'm not the only musician on this date, you know.”

Taylor smirked at my words. “Well, that may be true, but I’m not a performer. I don’t... I sing for me, you know? Not other people.”

“I get it. You like to keep some things to yourself,” I said as the waitress brought our drinks.

“Yeah, I do,” he said, and he took a sip of the foam on his Americano.

I noted that the brave souls who wished to be on stage had started to line up, so I excused myself, and Taylor only waved me off. But I could see the smile peeking at the corners of his lips as he did so, which only fueled me to do what I initially came here to do.

Because I hadn’t felt this inspired by anyone since...

Since ever, really.

My relationships fueled my songwriting, sure, but it wasn’t like I wrote songs about the beauty of love, or the levity of those feelings. No, like Taylor Swift, my flames all ended in catastrophe's, with Rozen throwing me and my shit out on the lawn as the biggest one. I knew the world was waiting for our 'break up song', but didn't have it in me to put any more emotion, any more energy, into Rozen fucking Lane. I wanted to move on from what had happened and I wanted more than ever to give Rozen the biggest *fuck you* of all and be happy.

Without him and his so called love.

I slid my phone out, pulling up my notepad as I anxiously awaited my turn to take the stage, my nerves starting to flare up.

I couldn't remember the last time I'd gotten nervous before I took the stage. I did it so often it was like breathing, but this... this was different. I wasn't singing, or performing covers. I was going to read the first poem I'd written in probably twenty years. And suddenly, the levity of that hit me just as I was called on stage.

Oh fuck!

I walked out, took my seat on the stool, the bright lights hitting me even though I was wearing shades. I opted to keep them on, if only to keep from going blind, but also because I truly felt it hit the beatnik vibe.

I took a deep breath as I looked at my phone, my palms sweating.

"He looks pretty under the moonlight

A fire burning bright

Petals that only bloom in the dead, dark night

He looks pretty against the dawn

Surrounded by the light of the sun

Vines and petals closing, waiting for the one

He looks pretty in the rain, when all the other flowers drown

Because he was born in a thunderstorm, and lightning is his crown

My pretty little flower."

DREW

I breathed out the words as I searched the crowd, feeling more vulnerable than ever, and it was both exhilarating and terrifying, but it made me feel alive.

And when my gaze fell on familiar blue eyes, I knew exactly who I'd written it for.

When I'd taken my seat back across from Taylor, I pushed up my shades on top of my head.

"Okay, be real with me, was it cringe?" I asked.

Taylor shook his head. "No, not at all. It was..."

I took a sip of my coffee, finishing the last bit.

"It was beautiful. I had no idea you wrote poetry," he said, dumbfounded.

"There's a lot of things people don't know about me," I said as the waitress came by with the check.

Taylor snatched it out of her hand before I could even look at it, regaling me with a stern look that immediately had my cock hardening again, and fixed me to my seat like a scolded child.

"You have done enough, let me do something for you," he said sternly.

"You already have, Taylor," I said, my heart in my throat.

Did he not understand that it was him who drove me crazy?

Inspired me to write again after so long?

That he was the reason I didn't want to end this perfect date, this perfect night...

This perfect few days.

"Not negotiable, Axel," he said as he placed his credit card on the dish, the waitress collecting it and scampering off. "Besides, you did say I could get the next one, and then you'd steamrolled me and the girls with a bottle of champagne and a night of binge drinking, so... consider us even, now."

Even, huh?

"Is that so?" I asked, a slow smile

spreading across my face.

"Because I rather like it when we're... unbalanced." I chose my words wisely.

I queued up my Uber, calling us a ride while Taylor signed his receipt, taking back his card.

When we'd finally gotten back to the pizza place, I'd fully intended to part ways and take the Uber back to the hotel, when Taylor suggested he could drive me.

A part of me, the celebrity part of me, had alarm bells going off left and right. Aside from rideshares, Helena usually transported me everywhere, and even when I was in relationships, my partners and I usually carpooled in limos or private cars where neither of us were driving.

The reality that I'd be alone in a car with a man I was heavily attracted felt like the most right thing in the world, but self-preservation made me nervous.

But I trusted Taylor, even though I knew it wasn't logical to.

So, I said yes.

And the entire ride back to the Paradise, I couldn't take my eyes off of him, how the moonlight really did light him up as we drove through the quiet streets of Jasper Springs.

That was the moment I knew.

That this wasn't just some wild mid-life crisis moment, not some mental breakdown, and not some song-writing fodder for my next album.

I was falling in love with the small town florist who loved iced coffee, Taylor Swift, and who made me feel like in a room full of people like I was the only one in the room.

But I couldn't find the words to speak.

Instead, all I could do was string them together in my head like little melodic puzzle pieces.

Driving in your car, watching you sing

Wrap a ribbon around my heart baby, it's a god damn scene

DREW

I think I love you and I don't know what that means

For me, for you, for the future unforeseen.

When we finally pulled into the parking lot, neither of us moved. We sat there for what felt like an eternity until one of us spoke, and it was me.

"Well, thanks for the ride, I hope you had a good time," I said, reaching for the door.

Taylor's fingers gripped the steering wheel. "Wait," he said, turning the car off, and climbing out. I did the same, coming around to the front of the car to meet him.

"At least, um, let me walk you to the door?" he said softly.

I could tell by the way he held his shoulders, by the tone of his voice, something was bothering him, but I didn't want to press. Maybe he just didn't want this perfect night to end either, and I couldn't blame him.

He looked pretty in the moonlight, a fire burning bright

Petals that only bloom in the dead, dark night.

I didn't want to waste another moment, so I took the moment and made it mine.

I set my hand on his hip, pulling him close, and to my surprise, he relaxed, his entire body *sinking* into my hold like it was home.

"I'd like that," I said, my voice full of breathy desperation. "I like *you*," I said, the words heavy in the air between us as I leaned my forehead against his.

Taylor's fingers found their way into my hair as he pulled me closer, bridging the gap between us with finality as his lips took mine.

He kissed me with a feral heat, a hunger that only stirred my insides, my blood, like a hurricane.

I kissed him back with my own feverish need, relishing in the taste of his tongue in my mouth, a deep groan escaping my chest as he gripped my hair, his free hand settling on my hip, squeezing it.

I could feel his welcome hardness against my own, the crisp wind chilling my skin as heat blossomed between us.

When he broke away, he whispered, "I like you too."

Though this whisper was full of fear, of uncertainty, and all at once, I wrapped my arms around him, holding him close as I tried to quell the pain he felt.

Whoever had hurt him, hurt him good, but I didn't want him to hurt any longer.

"I wanted to do that all night," Taylor whispered, biting his lip, which was pleasantly swollen from our kiss.

"Me too," I said as I took his hand in mine.

Taylor smiled under the artificial lamp

light as we walked slowly to the underpass of the Paradise, the bright lights of inside calling me.

But I didn't want to venture into Paradise alone.

"Stay," I whispered as I pulled him into my arms again, running my hand through his silky hair, gazing into his sapphire eyes.

He looked at me, biting his lip as he nodded. "Okay."

CHAPTER TWENTY-SIX

Taylor

MY HEART BEAT like a thunderstorm in my chest as I followed Axel up to his hotel room.

There was nothing to blame my actions on now, no alcohol, no 'it's not me its you', bullshit.

And after everything that had happened, after a night that was so unbelievably perfect, after I'd watched him spout fucking poetry over coffee… I couldn't deny the truth any longer.

The truth was I didn't just like Axel.

I *loved* him.

I loved how he held a guitar, how his eyelashes stood out against this pale skin, that he had covert Swiftie tattoos, wrote poetry, and I really, really loved how he could push my buttons in just the right way, to make me feel alive and wanted.

But falling for anyone, musician or not, was terrifying for me. I was worried I'd end up broken hearted again, and this time I might not be as easily mendable.

But I also knew that I didn't want to go home alone. Not without him, but I was acutely aware that this moment was going to change everything.

Because I knew what I wanted, and for the first time in my life, I felt like I could reach out and touch it.

Like I could truly *have it.* Even if it was just for a night.

The familiar words of Taylor's *Wildest*

DREW

Dreams about seeing me again and wildest dreams echoed in my brain as I followed Axel up the steps, down the hallway, and into his hotel room. The door closed and not a moment later had the storm commenced.

I pulled Drew to my lips once more, savoring the taste of him.

He wrapped his hands around my waist, pulling me closer as we stumbled through the hotel room like two drunken idiots, only this time we were the furthest thing from drunk.

We were both stone cold sober.

"We don't... have to..." he breathed into my mouth as I tugged at his shirt.

"I know," I breathed back as he removed his shirt to reveal his slick, defined chest with the smattering of tattoos stemming from his shoulders. "But I want this," I said, taking in the sight of him.

The next words to fall out of my mouth

were the final crack in my armor.

"I want you, Axel."

Something shifted in his eyes, the moment the words were in the air.

All the air was sucked out of my system as he took not one, but two steps closer, placing both his inked hands on the sides of my face, kissing me with ferocity, and passion as he whispered, "I want you too, Taylor."

Fire roared within me, ignited by his words, flipping a switch no one else ever could and I suspected, never would again.

"Oh yeah?" I said haughtily, his hands making quick work of unbuttoning my pants. My dick twitched at the sudden movement, the feel of his palm against my cockhead as he slid my boxers and pants down to the floor.

"Is this what you want, Axel? Hmmm?" I asked as I thrust myself against his hand.

"Yes," he breathed desperately, his

hands settling on my hips as he ground his own hardness against me.

I ripped at his buttons, his zipper, finding his steely cock hard and ready for me. I stroked the velveteen shaft slowly, letting my fingers tweak the steel studs, watching his entire body shudder as I did so.

"Yes, what?" I said as I squeezed him tight, feeling emboldened by his words, his reaction to my touch.

He was so responsive to me, and it was addicting.

"Yes, sir," he purred as he pulled at the hem of my shirt, thrusting himself in my hand.

I could feel the faint beginnings of his precum coating my fingers, and I groaned in response as my own cock twitched.

I pushed him back against the bed, watching as he fell like a domino against the stark white sheets. He gazed up at me, long eyelashes fluttering, his heavy, sizable cock on display bouncing back and forth. Though he did not touch himself, not even once.

He only stared up at me with wonder, watching, waiting for my next move.

For me to instruct him.

For me to take control.

I didn't have a lot of *experience* in that department, being as my sexual partners weren't into much else other than the basics, but a part of me wanted to explore this new side of me.

The side only this man was capable of bringing out.

I grabbed my own cock, stalking closer. If Drew liked me... *degrading...* I could channel my inner grouch. Or at least I could try.

"What makes you think you deserve this cock, huh?" I said as I gave my length a long, lazy stroke. I didn't miss the way his pupils dilated, how his swollen cockhead glistened in the light, how his thighs tightened as he tried *not* to thrust against the air.

"I don't..." he said, biting his lip. "I really don't, but..."

"You're right... you don't, you... you..." I searched my brain for the right word, settling on it, but it still felt awkward to say because I wasn't used to it.

A steady pause filled the space as I licked my lips and let out a steady breath.

"Manwhore," I said, my gaze searching his for approval, understanding. Drew's eyes sparkled, and I felt a breath of relief as I knew I was on the right track.

So far so good...

"I am a whore," he responded darkly, his wicked smile causing my cock to throb. "I'm your whore," he said, his voice full of lust and darkness.

I leaned on the bed, bracing my knees at his sides, straddling him so our cocks were both front and center. The bed creaked with my added weight as I grabbed both of us in my hand.

Drew's head fell back in ecstasy as he cursed.

So, I kept going, because it felt good. Cathartic even.

His cursing, the feel of his skin against mine, the sense of power washing over me that I did this to him.

I made him come undone.

"That's right, *Axel*, you're mine," I breathed, the words like a spell I never wanted to break. I stroked us both in my fist, building a steady, torturous rhythm.

"But I want you to show me just what an *experienced* little whore you are," I grunted, high off the ecstasy of this new power dynamic.

All at once, I released him, pulling him against me as we rolled so that I was now underneath him, his steel-piercings grinding against my leaking cock. The feel of his weight against me, of his piercings kissing my sensitive skin, of my hands running over his muscles just felt so... right.

Perfect.

I wrapped my legs around his hips, locking my ankles together as he braced himself with his elbows on the sides of my head. He ran a hand through my hair, green eyes ablaze with wonder and love.

And I was overwhelmed by him, by the sight of such illustrious, precious things.

"Are you sure?" he asked shakily, breaking character.

I shifted my hips, using my heels to dredge him closer to my entrance, knowing full well what I was asking and that this was it.

There was no going back after this.

But a part of me wanted to break, to know I'd been touched by such a force.

I nodded, my breath catching in my throat. "I'm sure," I said, and I pressed my mouth to his, stroking his tongue with mine as I ground my leaking cock against his firm belly.

Axel leaned back on his knees for a moment, unlocking my grip around his hips. He leaned over swiftly, grabbing a bottle of travel lube from the drawer, and I watched with my heart in my throat as he poured it in his hands, rubbing it all along his fingers, all over his length. When he leaned forward again, he kissed me, welcoming my legs back around his hips as his fingers breached my tight hole, slowly, coolly.

I gasped from the sensation of the coolness, the sudden intrusion. It'd been a long time since I had anyone's fingers in my ass but my own.

"Breathe, baby. Just breathe," he whispered, his voice catching.

I let out a slow breath, my body adjusting to him as he built a slow and steady rhythm. In, out, in out.

"That feels good," I whispered, closing my eyes in ecstasy as he slid another finger in.

My legs tightened around him as I started to rock against him, my cock throbbing with need at that point as it rubbed against his hard abs, leaving wet, sticky precum trails along his skin.

Drew pulled me back in for another fiery kiss, his fingers vacating me.

There was a steady pause as he lined himself up, his thick, slick head pushing into me slowly, inch by inch.

My body opened up to accommodate him, but the stretch was more than noticeable, and once he was in...

My insides clenched around him as I adjusted to his girth, and his steel.

It seemed like an eternity that we laid there, still and unmoving, locked around one another, me holding onto him for dear life, nothing but the sounds of our labored breath in the silent forever.

He moved slowly, and I arched my back to meet him as we both found uncharted territory, together.

"Mine," he whispered against my lips as he kissed me, slowly thrusting himself inside me.

My mind and my body splintered into a thousand, broken little pieces as his steel dragged over my sensitive nerves, making me see white. I nodded as I kissed him back, my right hand seeking purchase in his hair, my left settling at his back, pushing him further into me as he bottomed out, a deep unrelenting growl escaping his lips, pushing me over the edge into oblivion.

I thrust my cock against his stomach, coming without warning as he pulsed inside me, filling me with his own searing release. I moaned into his mouth as my orgasm ransacked me, making my entire body shiver and convulse around his pulsing cock.

My fingers dug into his back as I made my way to the heavens and back down again, into the safety and sanctity of his arms as he held me tight against his warm chest.

And when he finally vacated me, the last bit of me shattered along with his escaping release, and I knew I was surely doomed.

Because without a doubt, I was in love with Drew Axel.

And that changed everything.

CHAPTER TWENTY-SEVEN

Drew

TWENTY MINUTES UNTIL show time.

For an impromptu concert in an outdoor setting, I was impressed with the turnout. It seemed Howler's social media "Drew Axel Uncovered" flash concert campaign featuring my covers was actually something folks showed up for in spades.

I'm sure the fact it's a free concert probably helped too.

I strummed a few chords, making sure everything was a go, letting myself get carried away.

All day, I'd been humming the unrecorded melody in my head as lyrics danced around.

Like a flower in the breeze, like coffee with just the right amount of cream

Baby, I was made for you, and you

You were tailor made for me...

I slid out my phone, noting the chord progression, smiling as the words came so easy now.

But that wasn't the only reason I couldn't stop smiling.

It might have had something to do with waking up next to Taylor as he curled into my chest, or it might have had something to do with the hot shower we'd both ended up in that morning, which turned out to be the dirtiest shower ever. My skin might have been cleansed, but my ass was still a little on the sore side.

DREW

But I had to admit, *Sir* was a good persona for him, and I didn't mind his taking control one fucking bit.

In fact, I kind of loved being at his mercy. I got the gist that the role was a pretty new experience for him, and I was intent on providing as much support and encouragement as I could, because damn, did he do it *well.*

Though there was the impending departure dampening all my wishes and dreams, as I had at least two more scheduled shows to perform before I'd have to be back in LA to meet up with the band and discuss our next album together.

I knew it would be a long shot—and after Taylor's opening up to me, I knew that this was territory I'd have to tread lightly. The last thing I wanted was for my new...

Were we dating?

I knew it was more than fucking

around, but we hadn't really discussed labels or exclusivity. But I knew that what we had was undeniably something more than friends with benefits. I wanted us to be a thing. I hoped he wanted that too.

You miss one hundred percent of the shots you don't take, Axel.

For some reason my high school Prom fuck's words echoed in my brain. I'd taken my shot with him, in the back of his pickup truck, but he'd shot me down because he was too scared for anyone else to know he was into dudes.

I'd always been one to take a chance, to take the risk. If I would have played things safe all those years ago, I would have never left Jasper Springs, and I'd probably still be here.

Which made me wonder how different my life would have been had I not signed that record deal.

Would Taylor and I have met?

Would we still have ended up tangled

up together in my bed if I wasn't a traveling rockstar?

Would we both be shacked up together in a little cozy cottage, making floral arrangements together?

I pushed the thoughts from my mind, knowing I needed to get my head focused on the task at hand. The concert.

Afterward, Taylor and I had planned to meet up for drinks at M's Place, and I figured then we could talk about us.

Or rather, how to proceed with the *us*, given my current schedule. I didn't expect the guy to uproot his life or anything, but I wanted to give things a real shot.

People had long distance relationships all the time, right?

I had just set down my American Vintage II amber and white stratocaster, when I heard footsteps behind me. Figuring it was one of the stagehands, I didn't bother to turn around until a voice called my name, making my blood chill.

"Hello, Drew." The sultry, pretentious tone pulled me from my thoughts, and I turned around in a rush.

Standing before me was America's Sexiest Man Alive, decked out in his shiny new Jimmy Choo's and his deep gray Balenciaga suit. He looked less like a businessman and more like a mob boss, but his stony gaze and perfectly golden complexion made him look like a poor replacement from those Fifty Shades of Gray movies.

"Rozen," I said, my tone clipped. "What the fuck are you doing here?"

True to his nature, his expression was unreadable as he cocked his head to the side, amber eyes making me see red as he looked at me like I was some imbecile.

"I see you are still upset, over our last meeting," he drawled with all the finesse of a snake.

"You mean when you threw me out of our house amidst a sea of reporters because I found *you* in bed with that half-brain co-star of yours." I crossed my arms. "Yeah, I suppose any man in their right mind would be salty about being thrown out of their own damn house."

Rozen took a step closer to me, and I tensed. His eyebrows furrowed, and he must have taken my flinch as something more desperate than what it was.

"We all make mistakes, darling. Surely you know that," he purred, reaching out to run his fingers along my cheek.

I swatted him away as I took a step back.

"Axel, darling…"

"No," I said. "You don't get to play these games, Ro. I'm not some suit you can wear whenever you fucking feel like it. I am a person, with needs, with—"

He grabbed my wrist, a sliver of his suit cuff bristling against my skin as his thumb stroked the underside of my wrist over my veins. His grip was firm, deliberate, and once upon a time, I'd lived for it.

For his order, his dominance.

But not anymore. If our split taught me anything, it was purely how naive I'd been to think Rozen Lane actually cared about me.

He only cared about the control—which was why I was on a strict diet, had damn near all the clothes in my closet pre-selected, and was constantly prepped on what to say and what not to say any time we made an appearance together.

And despite what others thought about our sex life, it was always one sided.

But I'd thought that was what I needed, at the time. I thought that was love.

Now, I knew better.

He pulled me closer with just one motion, and I hated it. He set his free hand on my hip, like a vice holding me in place.

DREW

"I miss you, pet."

"I can't do this, not now, not—"

The steel grasp of his hand on my chin turning my head happened so fast I barely had a second to process before he pushed the crushing weight of his lips against mine.

I'd kissed this man a hundred times over the course of our relationship—if you could really call it that—but those kisses had always left me wanting, waiting for something he was never truly capable of giving me.

But now... I felt nothing.

Nothing except the bristle of his dry lips as he tried to force his tongue in my mouth, and it made me want to throw up.

This isn't what I wanted anymore.

Rozen may have been America's Sexiest Man Alive, but as far as I was concerned he was America's Biggest Asshole, and he was no longer welcome in my mouth, or my life.

The audible gasp I heard sent a shiver up my spine as my bearings caught, and I pushed Rozen away.

My gaze fell on Taylor, dressed in his Sunday best khakis with a black button down, the sleeves rolled up. In his hands, he held a bouquet of all black roses, before he'd thrown them down on the dirt of the field.

"Taylor, wait..." I said as I reached out for him, shoving Rozen aside with a force I didn't know I possessed.

But it was too late.

I was too late as I watched Taylor's beautiful blue eyes water, as I watched his heart break before my eyes, just as he turned around and hightailed it out of there, leaving the black roses in the dirt along with his fragile heart.

"What the fuck are you doing here?" Helena said as she careened around the bend, looking between an escaping Taylor and a smug looking Rozen.

"Taking back what is mine," Rozen said coolly as Helena held up a hand to him. She took her stance between us, like a goblin against giants as she flashed her dark gaze at him.

"Last I checked, Drew Axel was a free range chicken, Old MacDonald, so that means you're fucking trespassing on a farm that no longer belongs to you."

Rozen slid his hands in his pockets, raising an eyebrow.

"Are you threatening me, Helena? Because one word to my assistant and I could have half of America raining on your little Black Parade."

I stepped in front of her, my eyes ablaze, my soul on fire.

"Get. Out," I growled. "Take your fucked up shit and destroy someone else, because I'm done, Rozen. With us, with you, and everything you stand for. If you don't want me to punch that million dollar face of yours square in your uninsured jaw, I suggest you turn around and walk out of here real fast and never ever speak to me or my team again. Do I make myself clear?" I said as my ear mic chirped with the warning for five minutes to show time.

Helena slid her arm around my waist, squeezing me.

"Crystal," Rozen said sourly, scowling at me in disdain. Once upon a time that look would have brought me to my knees, but not anymore.

I was worth more than the bullshit Rozen Lane told me I was worth.

And as I watched him leave, my heart shattered because even in our death he'd managed to rip apart the one thing in my life that had given me any semblance of salvation.

My eyes watered as I looked at the black roses, their dark petals blowing in the cool breeze.

"Axel, hey..." Howler's voice called me

from my spiral, and I glanced up at her.

"The show must go on," she said, her voice solid and even.

"Helena, I don't know if I can…"

"You can. You can and you will, because you're Drew fucking Axel, and you have an axe to grind."

I looked in the direction Taylor had run off, my heart in my throat.

"And I can't think of a better place to lay your heart out than on that stage, where thousands of people can see it for what it is."

But there was only one person who I wanted to see my heart for what it was.

"So you're gonna dry those eyes, you're gonna stand tall like the motherfucking badass I know you are, and you are going to knock them all dead. And then you're going to go after Little Shop Of Horrors, and you're definitely making him sign an NDA this time," she said with a smirk, and I couldn't help but laugh.

"What if he doesn't—"

"He will, Axel. But first..." She handed me my stratocaster, her gaze soft and understanding. "First you *sing.*"

I did as she said, wiping my eyes of my threatening tears, the countdown in my ears much slower than usual.

Ten, nine, eight...

And when I ran out onto the ball field, the bright lights shining on me and the roar of the crowd welcoming me once more, I knew I needed this.

I needed to put my pain, my words to the mic, to broadcast my feelings in a way I could never truly speak.

"Hey, how you all doing tonight?" I asked, forcing forward my Drew persona I'd crafted so well over the years, hiding behind his mask for just a moment in time.

And I sang my heart out to every Taylor Swift cover I'd planned to sing, hoping that somehow, somewhere, Taylor could hear them too.

Enchanted, Teardrops On My Guitar, Gorgeous, We Are Never Ever Getting Back Together, Wildest Dreams...

And when I took my final bow, I ran to find Helena, knowing exactly what I needed to.

CHAPTER TWENTY-EIGHT

Taylor

I JUMPED INTO my car, my hands shaking as I turned the keys in the ignition. My fingers gripped the steering wheel as I stared at the passenger seat where only a night ago Drew sat, sharing the space with me.

The lyrics of *All Too Well* blared through my speakers as Taylor crooned on about sweet dispositions and wide-eyed gazes while my heart thumped rapidly, my throat tight.

How could I have been so stupid?

Hadn't I learned my lesson the first time?

I smacked the steering wheel with frustration as the lyrics about translation and tearing up masterpieces blared from the car speakers.

I shut the radio off, because I just couldn't handle Miss Swift and her words that cut far too close for comfort right now.

Instead, I called Julie as I pulled out of the parking lot, wiping the tears that started to seep out of my eyes.

"Hey, Tay, how did it go at the concert?" she asked sweetly, and though I wanted to speak, all I could do was sob like an idiot.

"What happened?" she asked, her tone immediately shifting.

"He... I..." I couldn't even find the words, but I knew I needed to try.

"Rozen was there, and they were kissing... and..."

"Oh my God, Tay! I'm so sorry..." she said, going into damage control mode. "What do you need, honey?" she asked.

"I don't know, I just... it hurts, Jules. I thought—"

"I'm coming over," she stated definitively.

"No, I—"

"Not negotiable, Tay. I'm coming, and we're going to get through this, okay?" she said, and she hung up.

The melodies of Taylor started up again, as she cried about being a crumpled up piece of paper lying on the ground.

When I pulled into my driveway, Julie was already there, standing on my front porch with a tote bag full of food by her feet.

I climbed out of the car and walked slowly up the driveway.

She pulled me into her arms, and I couldn't help it. I cried like a fucking baby.

A part of me didn't want to believe what I saw was true. That it was all some misunderstanding, some romance novel trope where the two leads end up at the wrong place at the wrong time. But life wasn't some romance novel, and I knew better than anyone that relationships were complicated.

Drew might have told me he didn't intend on getting back together with his ex, but the darkest parts of my insecurity told me my anxiety was right.

I wasn't enough.

I was just some small town whim, not the Sexiest Man Alive.

I was just some hopeless romantic who'd fallen for a rockstar.

Julie's hands slid up and down my back as her voice soothed me.

I hugged her as I let the tears flow

unchecked as we stood there on my porch for what felt like forever.

We spent the rest of the evening watching Netflix, the cheesiest, dumbest romantic comedies that didn't take much brainpower, while gorging ourselves on ice cream. Though it was more me watching than anything, since Julie and Giselle seemed to be in a deep texting discussion half the night. But that was fine, since all I really wanted was to just... be. But company still helped make me feel less alone.

As I curled up under the blanket, my stupid heart still dared to dream about the man who'd crushed my heart, wondering what he would look like on my couch, sitting at my kitchen table with a cup of fresh coffee.

And just like that, the pain hit all over again.

But maybe this was what was meant to be. I never expected us to have a future, anyway.

I knew he'd get on his tour bus, leave, and I wouldn't be more than a memory.

"You really like him, don't you?" Julie finally asked, her voice calm and even.

"I fell in love with him," I said the words, for the first time out loud, and my heart skipped a beat.

Damn heart.

"Maybe you should talk to him. Get his story?"

I cast her a hopeful, sad glance. "Why, so he can tell me I'm not enough to my face?"

Julie scooted closer, throwing her arm around my shoulders.

"Tabloids are notorious for taking a picture and running with a narrative. All I'm saying is, maybe there's more to the story than what you saw."

"Maybe," I said with a sigh as I ran my hand over my eyes.

"All I'm saying is... don't pack up your

heart yet, Tay."

I sighed. "Okay," I said, if only because it was ten thirty, and I was exhausted. "I think, I should turn in. Thanks for coming over, but I'm beat," I said as I shut the television off.

It wasn't a lie, exhaustion had hit, and sleep seemed like a peaceful avenue to avoid the hope blossoming in my heart that Julie was right.

Maybe I'd been too quick to judge, but what did it matter now?

It wasn't like Drew was long for Jasper Springs. After this concert, he'd be off to the next one. So, I vowed that I would put Drew Axel out of my mind. I had a job to do, and I had a life to live, no matter how mundane or quiet it was, and I would find solace in that the same way I found solace when Zack left until I'd managed to put myself and my heart back together.

You're on your own, kid.

CHAPTER TWENTY-NINE

Taylor

AFTER A NEAR sleepless night, I was surely not running on enough coffee.

I parked my car outside the shop, taking a deep breath as I climbed out. I slid my key into the front door, but it seemed to already be unlocked.

A steady string of panic raced through me as I wondered if I'd left the place unlocked after I'd made Drew's black bouquet, cursing my inattentiveness because of the gothic heartthrob.

I pushed the door open, my eyes going wide at the sight before me.

Every surface, from floor to ceiling was covered in flowers.

Wreaths, vases, standing arrangements in a variety of flora, from hibiscus to roses to peonies and orchids...

Except for the slim, small path from the door that wound through the sea of flowers.

What the hell.

In the center of the room was a large heart-shaped arrangement made of Morning Glories.

Attached was a note. I walked up slowly, the sea of flora making it seem like my shop was a wonderland.

The lyrics of Taylor Swift's *Daylight* were scribbled on the paper, spots of ink blurred and smeared as if they'd been shattered by tears.

The soft strings of a guitar pulled my

attention as I turned my gaze to see Drew standing against the door to my office, ripped black jeans and a white fitted tee with a flannel that was blue.

Like morning glories.

"Like a flower in the breeze, like coffee with just the right amount of cream. Baby, I was made for you, and you... you were tailor made for me..." he sang softly, his vibrant green gaze catching mine as he strummed his guitar.

The sight of him amidst all the flowers, dressed down as he was, only made my heart lurch, made tears prickle my eyes.

I was frozen in place, staring at him like some fool as he took a step closer and continued to sing.

"And all my demons flee the room the moment I look at you, all the flowers rush into bloom," he sang, the melody soft, delicate.

"If I told you I loved you would you believe me? If I gave you the key to my heart would you free me from the dark? Because love never made me feel like a drowning sailor, love never felt so perfectly *tailored* for me..."

The tears escaped my eyes of their own volition, my heart lodged in my throat.

Drew took another small step, and another until the only thing that separated us was his guitar.

"Like a flower in the breeze, like coffee with just the right amount of cream. Baby, I was made for you, and you... you were tailor made for me..."

His voice wasn't dark or smooth, but instead raw and full of honesty. And in his eyes I could see the truth in the words he sang.

See the sadness and the longing, and my heart jumped, my hope getting the better of me.

"Taylor, I'm so sorry..." he said softly. "I never thought I'd see him again..."

"I know," I said shakily, my sweat

sinking into the paper I squeezed in my hands.

"He thought... he thought he could come back into my life like nothing had happened. But something *did* happen," he said, running a hand through his dark locks. His verdant gaze was glassy, and I noticed his hand was shaking.

"You happened, baby," he breathed out. "I fell in love with you, Taylor."

His words fell on me like a steel beam, crushing me with the levity of their truth.

"I love you too," I said through my own shaky breath, afraid if I blinked Drew and all the flowers would disappear.

That perhaps I was hallucinating.

Can this be a real thing?

He reached his hand out, stroking my cheek, and the touch was warm. He looked at me with tears in his eyes, and hope reared its warrior sword.

All the panic, the anxiety, the what-ifs...

None of it mattered, because when I looked at him I knew.

I knew he loved me, and that was terrifying on so many levels.

But so fulfilling too.

"I don't know how to do this," I said through a sob.

And in that moment, Drew slung his guitar around his back, and in one fell swoop, he pulled me into his warm arms, against his solid chest, and I couldn't hold back my tears any longer.

I wrapped my arms around him, holding him tight so I knew he was real. That he was really here in my shop, holding me. My fingers gripped the soft flannel as I buried my head against his chest.

"I know," he whispered, his fingers seeking purchase in my hair as he gently pulled my head back, forcing me to look at him.

"But we can figure it out. Together,

if..."

I watched him lick his lips, his dark gaze falling on me with so much hope and promise, it was difficult not to melt into a puddle on the floor.

"If that's what you want, Taylor. If not... just..."

I pulled his face to mine as I took his lips like a prayer.

I kissed him with all that I was, with every ounce of my being, that infectious hope blossoming like an orchid in the darkest of places.

His lips tasted of salty tears and bitter coffee.

"Yes," I said through a choked sob as he kissed me back, taking my face in his hands, his fingers sliding in my hair as he poured himself into me.

"How the hell did you get all these in here..." I said as I broke away, both our chests heaving.

Drew brushed some stray tears off my

cheek as he smiled, the corners of his eyes creasing just a hair.

"Okay, well... I *might* have had some help..." he said.

I raised an eyebrow, but I didn't move my hands from his hips.

"You mentioned Julie helped you sometimes, so... I called Giselle... who called Julie... who had a key..."

I closed my eyes as a tear-filled laugh escaped my throat.

So that's what had her so distracted.

The little devil!

"And... let's just say I owe Howler a bottle of Jameson and new buzz buzz," he said, flashing me with a sexy grin that could easily have landed him the title of Sexiest Man Alive.

"Do I even want to know what a buzz buzz is?" I chuckled.

"Probably not, but trust me when I say you're worth it."

The way his words penetrated my

heart was more than validating. It was worth more than a ticket to the Eras tour.

"And don't you forget it," I said, and I claimed his lips once more.

"Never, Taylor," he whispered over my lips as he pressed his mouth to mine.

I guess happy ever afters do exist after all.

EPILOGUE

Four Months Later
Taylor

M'S PLACE WAS hopping, thanks to the crowd for their usual Bar Bingo & Karaoke. Though crowds didn't seem to bother me as much as they used to anymore.

I dropped off our drinks at the table, with the help of Giselle's fiancé, Aaron.

With just two months left until Giselle and Aaron walked down the aisle, these wedding party hangouts were starting to become more of a frequent thing. And as Giselle's official florist for the wedding, she insisted I attend every function like I was part of the wedding party itself.

But if I had to be honest, I did actually enjoy it. Hanging out with her and her brother, Grayson, Julie, Leah, and the rest of the party, I no longer felt like I needed to be closed up all the time, which was a nice change, and with business picking up—from a viral TikTok of my Taylor Swift inspired bouquets, everything felt right.

Well, mostly right.

Drew was still out of town, and we hadn't quite nailed down his next visit yet, but thanks to modern technology— and quite a bit of phone sex—the long distance thing didn't seem as daunting as it once did. And despite my paranoia that reporters would show up on my porch any day, they hadn't.

DREW

"I can't believe in just two months we'll be walking down the aisle," Giselle gushed, her eyes full of that pre-wedding sparkle.

Aaron smirked. "I can't believe in two months we'll be on a plane to Cabo," he said, and he took a drink of his whiskey. "I'm dying for a fucking vacation after all this wedding planning stuff."

"True that," Julie said with a laugh. "I think we're all ready for a damn party." She giggled.

Leah was crooning out a rather tone-def rendition of Carrie Underwood's *Before He Cheats*, and I couldn't help but slightly cringe.

"I'll drink to that," I said as I raised my glass, everyone clinking theirs together in time. Then a familiar voice pulled my attention.

"You're getting up there tonight, right?"

I turned so fast, I nearly spilled my

beer. Drew stood before me, wearing one of his tight, form-fitting tees with his blue flannel, and a pair of blue jeans, and Converses.

My heart leapt at the sight, and I couldn't help that I nearly knocked over the chair, throwing my arms around him. He chuckled darkly as he set his hands on my hips, squeezing me like he too was afraid I'd disappear.

"I thought…"

"Let's just say I had some well-deserved vacay time coming my way." He smirked.

"How much vacation time?" I asked as I held him in front of me, running my hands up and down his arms, if only because I missed the feel of those hard, smooth muscles under my fingertips.

"Three months worth. Which means…"

"You'll be able to come to the wedding!" Giselle squealed, jumping up and down. Julie bounced with excitement too, and my heart lifted.

Three months.

Three perfect months with the man of my dreams.

Leah finished up her song, bounding back to the group, a look of excitement on her face as well.

"Pulling some big strings aren't you?" she teased Giselle, winking at me.

"Some of us know what's important," he said, flashing a grin. "Besides, I wouldn't miss G's wedding for anything. I know it's going to be epic, especially those floral arrangements," he said as he dramatically pretended to faint.

I hit him in the chest playfully. "You are insufferable," I growled.

Drew smiled at me wickedly. "Oh, you ain't seen nothing yet, baby." He leaned in, delivering a chaste kiss on my lips as the DJ called out the next singer.

"Taylor Meade? Is there a Taylor Meade in the house?"

I shot my boyfriend the dirtiest look, knowing full well he was going to pay for that later. But I couldn't very well leave him hanging, not after he flew all this way.

"You're going to pay for that," I said as I slid my hand in his, pulling him with me to the stage.

"Is this a duet now?" he teased.

I shook my head as I skipped up the steps with him following behind.

"If I'm going to sing like a canary, you best believe I'm going to need backup."

He squeezed my hand tightly, a dark chuckle escaping his throat.

"So demanding," he said playfully.

The lights were bright as I walked to the microphone, the beginning notes of Taylor Swift's *Mine* filling the space. I shook my head as he slid his hand around my waist.

"Like... so paying for this," I said with a grin.

DREW

Drew squeezed my waist. "I'm counting on it, sir."

I turned to the microphone, looking out into the crowd, feeling more alive than ever.

And I sang everything that was in my heart.

Mine.

Sick Little Games Song Lyrics

Axe 2 Grind

Tonight, I'll be the monster and you can
be my prey
Honey, I'll be the match, and you can be
my flame
Pour some gasoline on it, baby, let's play
some sick little games…
Baby, you can run but you can't hide, I
know you like the chase, I know you like
the ride, so I'll hunt you down, baby, I'll
show you how to slay, when you and I
play our
Sick little games

So bounce for me, bunny, show me what I
like
Shake your tail feather for me, honey,
primed for the fight
Tell me you want it while mascara runs
down your face
Tell me you want to play sick little games

Sick, sick

EVIE RILEY

Sick little games
Sick, sick
Sick little games
Pour some gasoline on it, baby
Watch us go up in flames
When you and I play our sick little games

It's 3 AM and the demons are awake
I can't stop thinking about you and our
Sick little games
You haunt me with your pretty eyes, and
the blood smeared across your face
Dragging me down with your sick little
Promises you made to me were in vain
You said you lived for our
Sick little games

Sick, sick
Sick little games
Sick, sick
Sick little games
Pour some gasoline on it, baby
Watch us go up in flames
When you and I play our sick little games

DREW

Run, run, run away, baby
The midnight hour is close at hand
The sun will come up and you'll leave me
again
Run, run, run away, baby, just as fast as
you can
911 call the doctor, I don't think I can
stand
Losing you, begging you, asking you to
stay
Stay, stay, stay
So we can play, play, play
Our sick
Sick little games

Thank you for reading Drew and Taylor's story.

If you enjoyed this book, please return to your favorite retailer and leave a review. Even a few words could mean the world to an author.

Continue the series with Grayson's story, Book 4 in Jasper Springs!

OTHER BOOKS BY EVIE

Federal Protection Agency
Mason
Rafe
Ryzen
Cooper
Noah
Damien
Sebastian
Gabe
Logan

Ruthless Empire
Courting Danger
Chasing Danger
Kissing Danger

Smokejumpers
Hawke
Cyrus
Jase
Gage
Jackson
Xavier

Jasper Springs
Cade
Dawson
Drew
Grayson
Riley
Mitch

From The Edge
Shattered
Runaway
Jaded
Rescue
Hidden
Tormented

Gray Vale Pack
His Fated Mate
His Wounded Warrior
His Healing Heart

ABOUT THE AUTHOR

Evie Riley is a prolific, neurodivergent author known for her captivating MM romance novels. She has gained a significant following and topped the LGBT+ action and adventure bestseller charts with her series.

Evie's writing style often explores dark and gritty themes where her men must overcome difficult obstacles in their search for love, but she has also ventured into sweeter small-town romances, incorporating tropes like enemies-to-lovers, friends-to-lovers, age-gap, and forced proximity. She is known for crafting engaging romantic suspense novels and has a knack for creating interconnected series worlds that keep readers invested.

EVIE RILEY

Interestingly, Ms. Riley has hinted at exploring new genres, such as Alien Omegaverse Romance, in the future.

Outside of writing, she enjoys spending time at the beach and has a quirky personality, described by her partner as ranging from cute to deadly, depending on her blood-chocolate levels.

Evie spends her nights writing bad boys in love, and her days wrangling the sweet boys she loves.